MISTWALKER

Other Books by Saundra Mitchell

The Vespertine

The Springsweet

The Elementals

Shadowed Summer

Defy the Dark

MISTWALKER

Saundra Mitchell

HOUGHTON MIFFLIN HARCOURT
Boston   New York

Irish traditional ballad "She Moved Through the Fair" collected by Herbert Hughes
in *Irish Country Songs* (London: Boosey & Hawkes, 1909).

www.hmhbooks.com

Text set in Dante MT

Library of Congress Cataloging-in-Publication Data

Mitchell, Saundra.

Mistwalker / Saundra Mitchell.

pages cm

Summary: Forbidden to set foot on her family's lobster boat after her brother's death, sixteen-
year-old Willa will do anything to help her grieving, financially-troubled family, even turn to the
weird Grey Man who haunts the lighthouse near her small Maine village.

ISBN 978-0-547-85315-4 (hardback)

[1. Lobster fishers—Fiction. 2. Family life—Maine—Fiction. 3. Blessing and cursing—Fiction. 4.
Soul—Fiction. 5. Murder—Fiction. 6. Maine—Fiction.] I. Title.

PZ7.M6953Mis 2014

[Fic]—dc23

2013004144

Manufactured in the United States of America

DOC 10 9 8 7 6 5 4 3 2 1

4500450478

For Carrie—my imprint buddy and my friend.

I wouldn't be here without you.

ONE

Willa

The hope was used up; all we had left was superstition.

That's why Seth Archambault took my place on my father's fishing boat. That's why I stacked egg-salad sandwiches in a cooler instead of pulling on my oil clothes.

"Bad luck to have a woman or a pig onboard," my father told me over dinner the night before. Mom didn't blink; she knew it was coming.

"Which one am I?" I asked.

Dad didn't answer. He drained his coffee, then drifted from the table. His weighted steps shook the floor as he jammed a baseball cap onto his greying head. Last summer, his hair gleamed copper, the same watery shade as mine.

Old-time navy tales said it was supposed to be bad luck to have redheads aboard too, but we Dixons had proved that wrong for years. Like a bunch of Down East Weasleys, we'd always been ginger. Even the black-and-white pictures in Gran's albums showed generations of freckles on milky faces and waved hair too in-between to be blond or brunet.

And let's be honest. We were moored when my brother, Levi, got shot.

He fell onto the boat. Into my arms. And he died on the dock. So, technically, our bad luck lately had nothing to do with red-heads, pigs, or women onboard the *Jenn-a-Lo*.

But it wasn't an argument I wanted to have before sending my father and my boyfriend into new October seas. That's why I got up with a dawn I couldn't see and made sandwiches I didn't like. Leaving through the back door, I kicked Levi's boots out of my way and headed for the water.

The fog cloaked me in dewy silk. It tasted cool and beaded in my hair. I moved through it uneasily. My walk was familiar, but the world was hidden—I held my hand out to touch everything I could to guide me.

At the end of my walk, the *Jenn-a-Lo* slept where she always did when we weren't fishing her. But she was a ghost in the mist; we all were. An unseen harbor bell called, answered by the sleepy bump of boats against their slips.

Conversations drifted in the air, disconnected from breath and body. But I recognized the voices—Mr. O'Toole wanted to know if Zoe Pomroy still had his coffee grinder. Mal Eldrich asked if it was cold enough for Lane Wallace, which got him soundly cursed because it was the 275th day that year he'd asked it, and he'd no doubt ask it for the remaining ninety.

This was Broken Tooth before fishing started for the day: the wharf alive with ordinary, daring men and women. They laughed and cussed and got ready to sail on seas that would be just as happy to swallow them as feed them.

More likely than not, this had *always* been Broken Tooth. For the Passamaquoddy who fished here first, then for the English and French and Scots-Irish who drove them out.

Funny thing was, it never used to be *this* foggy. We'd have some, but everybody talked about how Broken Tooth didn't get blessed much, but we got blessed with clear waters. Not anymore; seemed like it hadn't been clear since Levi died. It was our shroud.

With a heavy sigh, I hurried to the *Jenn-a-Lo*. At first, just the red script of her name floated up in the fog. Trailing my hand along the rail, the boat took shape. She wasn't new; she wasn't beautiful. I loved her all the same.

Thankfully, in the pale of a frosted morning, I couldn't make out the shadow of Levi's blood, stained into the warp of the wood dock. Before I could think about it, a hand reached out of the mist to take mine.

"Egg salad?" Seth asked.

"What else?" I said, and stepped onboard. Putting the cooler

3

down, I slid it across the deck with a firm shove, then turned to find him. He was a shadow in the haze, then suddenly a boy. My boy.

In my orbit, Seth touched me with hands just as certain as my steps toward the shore had been. Brushing my lips against his jaw, I curled closer to him so I could slip toward his mouth. His skin was cool; at first, he tasted of coffee and Juicy Fruit.

The second kiss, though, tasted like nothing but want. That was the beauty of a silver morning: it was possible to steal away with someone without moving at all.

When I broke the kiss, I pressed my brow to Seth's temple. "You better be careful."

"Always," he said.

"Make Dad eat," I went on.

Seth's breath spread heat across my cheek. "I'll ask him to, anyway."

"Don't feel bad if you're just changing water in the pots," I continued. "Or pulling seeders and v-notches. That's just fishing this time of year."

I felt him smile. "I've got this, Willa."

Of course he did. I knew he did. But I felt strangely stripped, knowing that I wouldn't be my father's sternman today. As fine a fisherman as Seth was, he didn't know the particular rhythms of our boat. Her quirks waited to catch him, as if winter seas weren't wicked enough. It was supposed to be clear and cold today if the fog ever lifted, but there was no accounting for the Atlantic's whim.

"Mind the hauler. It's sticky," I told him, and smoothed off his knit cap so I could run my fingers through his hair.

Seth bowed his head, catching me in another needy kiss. Possessive, his hand tightened on my hip, and I twisted my fingers in his hair. Selfishly, I wanted to leave him with an edge, troubled by a hunger he couldn't satisfy.

That was the one thing I was still sure of, that Seth Archambault wanted me more than he wanted anything else in the world.

Catching his lower lip between my teeth, I tugged it as I pulled away. And then I put my back to him, walking off as quickly as I could.

In my family, we never said hello or goodbye—another superstition. That one came from my mother's side of the family. Without hello, you couldn't mark a beginning. To avoid an ending, of course you went without goodbye.

Maybe whoever started it thought they could live forever. All they had to do was trick time into believing their lives were a single, uninterrupted moment.

They were wrong.

Bailey didn't come to a full stop in front of my house. Instead, she pushed the passenger-side door open and yelled, "Get in, loser!"

Running alongside her battered pickup, I threw my apron and rake inside. The truck picked up speed on the incline, and I lunged for the door. And there I was, hand on window frame, feet off the ground. For a second, I was flying. Then I was rolling like a loose marble into the truck's cab. I fell against the seat with a laugh.

"What, you're too good for seat belts now?" Bailey asked.

I made a point of shutting the door before bothering to belt in. "Well, yeah. You're still too good to get your brakes fixed."

"Always judging."

"That's what friends do," I told her.

It was easy to smile with Bailey Dyer. We grew up together, literally. We met when our mothers, best friends, had plopped us in the same crib. We entertained each other while they played pinochle.

If you start out sharing a diaper bag with somebody, it's easy to share everything else. Bailey knew to the minute when I got my first period. She came out to me before anyone else. It's not like our moms were shocked by either of those developments, but it was still nice to have a secret-keeper.

"So is Seth . . ." Bailey started, turning the radio down. She didn't finish the thought. It was a blank for me to fill in, offered smoothly.

"Yeah, he's out there." I put my feet on the dashboard and sighed. She knew I hated it; she'd listened to me rasp my throat raw over it last night. But that was last night, and by daylight, I had to be practical. "Not a lot to be done about it, you know?"

Bailey drummed the steering wheel. "You could kneecap him."

"You can't dance in casts, dude."

"Like you care about the fall formal," Bailey said.

"Seth does. I think he bought a ring."

She cut a look at me, her brown eyes sparkling. "You're going to say yes, right?"

The weight of the air changed around us. Finally, I said, "I don't know," and leaned against my window. Instead of saying something useless, Bailey raised her brows and nodded, focusing on the rough road.

It was junior year, the deciding year. I'd planned to take the SAT with Bailey, just to lend her moral support. College had never been in my plans. I was going to marry Seth and fish with my father until he was too weathered to go out. Then the boat would be mine, then my kids', then theirs . . . It was a good life, a beautiful inevitability.

And it was gone.

A little farther down the road, Bailey asked, "Why not?"

"I can't." I said. "I've been paying the mortgage, Bay. Dad hasn't been out since Levi died. What if he never gets back out there proper?"

"He's fishing today." Bailey threw her shoulders back. "Okay, I know, with *Seth*. But if he won't take you out, buy your own boat. Pay their mortgage and yours, too . . . oh."

"Hey, look," I said, plucking my roll of apron and rake off the seat. "Mud flats."

Bailey dropped out of gear, then put all her weight onto the brake. We rolled to a stop on the gravel shoulder. The engine shuddered, making the whole truck shake before it finally went silent.

The old girl was a junk heap, and Bailey would have been better off buying a new one. But she was saving for college. Finessing another four thousand miles out of a Ford that should have been put down was a matter of pride.

We had that in common.

I got to the back first, unhitching the thing to get to our digging gear. The tailgate fell, rusty flakes fluttering to the ground as we pulled on rubber waders and tied each other's aprons. The former were necessary, the latter an in-joke.

They were our freshman home-arts project: uneven gingham monstrosities that would have made our grandmothers roll in their graves. Our aprons were thin and threadbare. Even if they weren't, fact was, nothing was going to keep us clean.

Snatching up our rakes and buckets, we started down the rocky incline to the shore. Low tide had taken the water out, leaving a gleaming expanse of grey mud. Thin-boned pine trees sheltered us from the wind; this cove was a good place to go digging because of that. With the tree break, the cove stayed a little warmer a little longer. If we were lucky, we'd have until the end of October.

Mussel shells decorated the flat, black and white bouquets that could cut as clean as a knife. Bailey walked down a few yards so we wouldn't get in each other's way, and we got to work. Piercing into the mud with my rake, I flipped it and reached in with bare hands. Nothing. Breath frosting in the air, I moved up and started a new row.

"First!" Bailey cried.

I looked over, and she held a bloodworm high, presenting it to me with a smirk. The little monster twisted on itself, trying to get its black teeth into her wrist. Bailey dropped it into her bucket and said, "That's what you get for changing the subject. I win, you lose."

"I like how classy you are," I replied. "All class, that's you."

Slapping her own butt, Bailey left a handprint. "Kiss it, Dixon."

I flicked a handful of mud in her direction, then went back to digging. Bloodworms didn't look like much, but on a long low tide, we could each pull three hundred. At a quarter apiece, that added up. For Bailey, her college fund. Lately, for me, the bills my parents couldn't manage.

"So . . ." Bailey dared again, because she was my best friend and knew she could get away with it. "How far out are they gonna have to go, do you think?"

"A ways." Cutting mud and pulling worms, I didn't lift my head, but I did raise my voice so Bailey could hear me. "Looks like those mokes on Monhegan aren't the only ones on winter lobster this year, I guess."

"You remember that one girl?" The *from Monhegan* was implied.

I pulled a worm, dumping it in my bucket. "Yep. Crazy like everybody else out there."

"You ain't lying," Bailey replied.

And then, because I could, in the middle of a mud flat, just the two of us and nobody else, I dared to say a wish out loud. "After this summer, we need a good season."

Bailey hauled her boots from the mud and moved to a new patch. Invoking casual magic, she said, "Ask the Grey Man. It can't hurt."

A ghost, or a revenant, maybe a cursed sailor or faery—who, or what, the Grey Man was was up for debate. People couldn't even agree that it was a man. Some of the old-timers insisted it was a Grey Lady.

But we all agreed that he lived in the lighthouse on Jackson's Rock, and if you could get him on your side, you'd have the best fishing of your life.

It was a lot like the Norwegians biting the head off a herring, or throwing the first catch back for luck. Chewing on anise and spitting on the hooks. Leaving women behind and never setting sail on a Friday. Old rituals we kept to guarantee the impossible: all good weather, no bad days.

But in our bones, we knew it was blizzards and nor'easters and squall lines that sank ships. Draggers and trawlers and people from away stealing our catches and leaving nothing for our pots. Government dopes making us trade float line for sink line, twice as expensive, lost twice as much.

In lobstering, nothing was certain—except the lighthouse on Jackson's Rock. And that was automatic and empty. If there was a Grey Man, he had lousy taste in real estate. No one went to Jackson's Rock and likely no one ever would. Just thinking about it made my head hurt.

Then again, maybe he was right where he meant to be— where no one could ask him a favor. Where he'd never have to grant one. Like most faery stories, the price was probably too high. My family had paid enough for our calling this year.

We couldn't spare anything else.

After selling my catch at the worm cellar, I wasn't ready to go home yet. The ocean flowed with new colors, crimson and gold. Sunset transformed the shore. It called the sailors and the fishermen home.

Pushing my hands into my back pockets, I walked down the dock. It was easy to tell who'd gone far out, past the island, halfway to Georges Bank. Nothing held their berths at the pier but short, choppy waves. No sign of Daddy and Seth yet either.

Lobsters liked warm water—that's why summer fishing was easy. As the seasons changed, they marched to the depths. They were safer away from shore. The rest of us, not really. Cold, open waters, waiting for drowning storms . . .

I wasn't gonna think about that. Once everybody came home safe, that would be the time to think dark thoughts.

Lifting my face to the wind, I walked over warped wood. Maybe it was crazy, but I loved the way it tilted beneath my feet. Being able to walk over it without looking filled me with a strange sense of pride. Like it was proof I belonged there. That this was my place and my destiny.

"That you, Willa?" Zoe Pomroy asked.

I couldn't see her, but it was easy to follow her voice. Turning down her slip, I approached the *Lazarus,* following the scent of coffee to the teal and white boat all the way at the end. That was the only place it fit.

Zoe had one of the bigger ships in our fleet. Fifty foot, with what amounted to an apartment inside. She had a kitchen and a head, a cabin and a guest room. When the weather was good, Zoe lived aboard. Daddy liked to give her hell about fishing from a yacht, but I admired her.

Leaning over the rail, Zoe grinned down at me. "I got something good today."

"What's that?" I asked, already climbing aboard.

Lamps illuminated the cabin. Everything inside gleamed, dark wood polished to a sheen. From the stern, I could make out the galley and the table. The rest of Zoe's floating condo required an invitation.

"I've been pulling traps for damn near thirty years," she said, opening a cooler on deck. She reached inside, hefting a lobster out with her bare hands. Its claws were already banded, so the worst it could do was wriggle at her. "And I've never seen one of these."

In the dimming dusk, it was hard to make out what kind of wonder she had. The lobster was kinda big, but nothing special.

Then Zoe dipped him into the light that spilled from the cabin. A spark of excitement raced through me. He was blue. Not kinda sorta, if you squint at a green lobster, you might see some bluish spots. No, this was a deep shade, halfway to navy. Midnight freckles and powder blue joints, even his eyes were a hazy shade of midnight.

"Hot damn, Zoe, that's something else."

"Isn't it?"

More than a little irritated—he'd probably been passed around to half of Broken Tooth by now—Old Blue the lobster curled his tail under. Flailing his claws, he wanted to pinch me. He just couldn't. I trailed a finger down his segmented tail and hefted him in my hand. He was eight pounds, easy.

"You taking him back?" I asked.

Nodding, Zoe leaned against the rail. "Yeah. He's bigger than legal, but I wouldn't have kept him anyway."

She didn't have to explain. Lobsters like these, we shared them. Took pictures, handed them around. Then we gave them back to the ocean. It balanced things; it reminded the water gods and the universe that we appreciated all of it. That we weren't so greedy to keep every last creature we pulled in our traps.

And it meant somebody else might find him later. Nobody knew how old a lobster could get. In fact, left alone, they might live forever. Every year, they shed their shells and grew a new one. Nothing limited how big they could grow.

Up in Nova Scotia, they found one that weighed forty-four pounds. Forget losing a finger to a lobster—that thing could break arms with its claws.

So if we gave back the big ones, the blue ones, the ones that were special, there was a little bit of immortality attached to it. In two days, or two hundred years, somebody else might haul it up. Take pictures, pass it around. Past to present, lobsterman to lobsterman.

I watched Zoe put Old Blue back in the cooler. "You see Dad and Seth out there today?"

"This morning," she said. Straightening, she dried her hands on her jeans. Nodding toward the cabin, she invited me inside. "Past the Rock, heading on out. You want some coffee?"

Back home, the house sat empty. Mom was at work, and Daddy was still out. There was nothing in that house but unnatural quiet, so I took a cup of Zoe's coffee, and another one after it. Just to stay on the water a little longer.

Just to be close to the sea.

ONE

Grey

Someone out there is thinking about me.

I feel it, as surely as I feel the wrought-iron stairs shake beneath me. It's a quickening, a bright silver sting that plays along my skin. It bites, it taunts. I measure my breath and hurry downstairs in spite of it. Or because of it. I don't know anymore.

The brick walls around me weep, exhausted from keeping the elements outside, but it's only fair. I'm exhausted too. I hold off a great deal more than wind and salt spray.

As ever, the table is set with linens and silver. As ever, the candles are lit. My prison is an elegant one. I don't remember when that started to matter.

When I was alive, I hated shaving each morning. I hated vests and breakfast jackets, cuff links, tie tacks, looking presentable. Now they're ritual. Acts I perform as if I could walk back into my world at any moment. And I can't. I never will.

Not even if she is thinking about me.

Sinking into my chair, I tell myself very firmly: stop wondering about her. Her thoughts aren't formed. They aren't real yet. She's not a possibility; this is not the end. And if I've learned one lesson in one hundred years, it is this: anticipation is poison.

So, instead, I consider the wrapped box at my place. It, too, is elegant—gold board, gold ribbon, a sprig of juniper berries for color. There's a clockwork movement inside, the heart of a music box.

If I assemble it correctly, it'll play the "Maple Leaf Rag." Carved lovers will spin around each other; silk maple leaves will wave. A merry addition to my collection.

I put the gift aside. And between blinks, my plate fills with salt cod and cream. This is my least favorite breakfast, and it's my fault I'm having it. Some girl and her unborn wishes distracted me, so I forgot to want baked apples and oatmeal. Or broiled tomatoes on toast. Or anything, really—birthday cake and shaved ice, cherries jubilee, Irish coffee and hot peppers.

Tomorrow, the gift box will have silk leaves in it, and galvanized casing nails so I can finish my music box. The day after, four new books on any subject, none of which matter, as long as I haven't read them before. They'll appear on my plate, then make way for my breakfast. This will happen again at noon and at five. Lunch and dinner.

They're regular as the clock I built, a mechanical sun chasing the moon across its face. It never slows. It never stops. I hear it toll every hour of every day as it marks the minutes to the next meal, the next box filled with nearly anything I desire.

And it doesn't matter that, lately, I let those boxes pile up in my study, unopened. Nor does it matter that I take one bite and wish my plates away. Sighing, I unfold my napkin and consider my silverware an enemy.

In the end, I'm afraid, it's a curse to get everything you want.

TWO

Willa

Since she was caught up worrying about the SAT instead of paying attention, Bailey stepped on the back of my shoe again. I stopped in the middle of the walk. As I expected, she kept going and crashed into me.

All betrayed, she asked, "What?" like I'd pulled a gun and rolled her for her iPhone.

"We're not sitting the test until May," I told her.

"But I have to be ready by then. You don't just waltz into the Ivies, Willa. I have to think about it now." Bailey waved her hands. "I don't even have a subject. I need one for apps, and you know I suck at essays. I don't get along with them, Willa! I choke!"

I stepped to the side so she could walk with me to school.

"Write about lobstering. Or growing up all quaint and whatever. Hell, write about being the only lesbian in a fishing village!"

"I'm not the only one," she said.

"Cait lives in Milbridge," I replied.

Folding a stick of gum into her mouth, Bailey shook her head. "It's not interesting. Dear Harvard, I'm unique and not a soul is bothered. Boo hoo hoo. Love, Bailey."

I wrinkled my nose. "You're not applying to Harvard."

"That's not the point!"

With a huff, Bailey picked up the pace. I gladly followed, because we were both going to be late the way we were dawdling. It's not like it was a long walk. The Vandenbrook School was our town school. K through 12 went there, to this Victorian mansion perched on a hill.

Mom said when she and Dad went to Vandenbrook, they had to climb uneven granite stairs set into the dirt. Talk about a mess of fun in the winter. Sometimes it would get so cold, the earth would spit one out like a baby tooth.

But right before I started kindergarten, the town trust paid to pave the walk. They even put warmers beneath the concrete to keep it clear. Come December, we'd be tromping through knee-deep snow to get anywhere except school.

Everybody argued about why they did it and how they found the money for it. But I guess people were making noises about busing us to Narraguagus, and pride set in. Like everything else in Broken Tooth, it came down to tradition—we always had schooled our own, and we weren't about to stop without a fight.

I liked it. I liked that I could find the place my dad scratched his initials in the old servants' stairs when he was seventeen and sick of school. My granddad had done the same, and his father, too, back when it was just ten boys taking lessons with the rich owner's son.

That wood contained one slice of me, the same way the *Jenn-a-Lo* claimed one, and the coast, and the jack pines, and the sea. I had planned to wait until graduation to add my initials. Instead, I broke in this past summer, the day of the funeral, to do it. It was too sunny outside, but nice and dark in the back hallway.

Bailey snapped her fingers in front of my face. The crack dragged me out of my thoughts, and I cooled my cheeks with my hands.

"Sorry."

"Where'd you go?" she asked. She clasped the back of my neck and pulled me in roughly. It wasn't a hug. It was a good shake, but it meant the same thing. I leaned into her, long enough to get her perfume on me, then threw my shoulders back.

"I'm all right."

"Yeah?"

"Yeah." And to prove it, I tugged my bag onto my shoulder

and said, "I think you should write about worm digging to pay for college. Make up some stuff about how cuts and worm bites get you good and tough. Ready for the world."

"Yeah, right."

"It doesn't have to be true," I told her, and started up the stairs. "It just has to get you by."

Some days pretended to be normal.

Because our school was a mansion once, it had good places to sit. The elementary kids hung out in the solarium. They were allowed to run in there and get their ya yas out. Plus, it let them soak up what little sun made it through the trees up here.

The foyer was for us, the high school kids. When I walked in, Seth had already staked out our favorite corner. The far edge of the window seat, where the light was the warmest. Great, weighted oaks cast their shadows, and by lunch, the foyer was dark. In the morning, though, it was quiet and kinda pretty.

Sliding into Seth's lap, I looped his arms around me the way I always had. Solid and warm, he melted to match me. He rested his chin on my shoulder, brushing his nose behind my ear. Everything fit.

"Morning," he murmured. His voice buzzed on my skin.

"Yessir, it is," I replied.

Seth smiled. He always did when I played literal with him. Holding me tighter, he fell quiet. He shifted and twitched beneath me. Fighting back a smile, I let him squirm. He was waiting for me to ask how it went with Daddy, and I wasn't about to. It was a sore subject, and anyway, he was going to tell me whether I asked or not.

"Yesterday was good," he finally said.

Reaching back, I trailed my fingers through his hair. "Catch anything?"

"Nope."

It wasn't a surprise. The traps had been out too long. Yesterday was an exercise in baiting and dropping, a chance for Daddy to get used to a sternman who wasn't a Dixon. I tried to push that aside. Twisting to look at him, I asked, "Everything run smooth?"

There was a hitch in Seth's answer, a little hesitation. "He kept coming on deck. I know how to gaff a buoy, but he kept wanting to show me."

Secretly, that made me feel good. When I was on the *Jenn-a-Lo*, Dad barely slowed down between traps. It was up to me to keep up. And I had no problem doing it. There was nothing better than hauling a string in record time. Well, if the pots were all full, that made it a little bit better.

To soothe Seth, I turned in his lap. Draping my arms over his shoulders, I tugged at the short hairs on the back of his neck. I kissed his downturned mouth and ignored it when one of the Eldrich boys hooted from the stairs.

"You did good, though."

"Think so?"

I nodded, our lips skimming when I spoke. "I do. And when you go out Wednesday, just tell him to get his ass back in the cabin where he belongs."

Seth snorted. "That's gonna go over."

"It will with me."

He'd known me my whole life. So he knew when he could pick me up. Picking up meant spinning. Used to be, I'd press my face against his neck. Breathe his after-shave and get my thrills from the smoothness of his smooth skin. All of a sudden, though, whirling in the foyer seemed like too much.

"Stop. Enough," I said, and I wasn't laughing like usual.

To his credit, Seth did. He tipped me so I could hop to my feet again. There was a space between us, one I filled by brushing my hair back and staring at the floor. In all the spots inside me that happy tried to fill, guilt pushed it out. I couldn't be playing at school. Laughing and copping feels. I just couldn't.

Looking past Seth, I stared down the hall. It was full, and one of the kindergarteners, Kenzie Fisher's kid sister, skidded along the slick floor. She crashed into Kenzie's legs. Without warning, Kenzie hauled her up and tossed her over her shoulder. Fat cheeks turned red, and the little Fisher's eyes bugged out.

There was only ever two years between me and Levi. I couldn't have held him upside down if I wanted to. But stupid me, stupid, irrational me—right then, I wanted to, so bad. Seth's rough hand skimmed across the back of my neck. Leaning over, he kissed my hair. He turned me, subtly, because he knew me too well.

"It's okay," he murmured.

It wasn't, but I said "I know" anyway.

With a pair of metal cutters in one hand, I turned my bead tray with the other. Somehow, I was supposed to turn a spool of wire and about fifty million little glass spheres into a bracelet, one with "depth" and a "point of view."

No idea what that meant, so I started with blue beads and figured I'd throw some silver ones in to go with.

If anybody asked, I was going to say it represented the Milky Way. The way it looked on a lightless, cloudless night, when we were halfway to Georges Bank. There, surrounded by sea and not a thing else, you were a real tiny slice of infinity. From there, you could see the shape of galaxies, silver and flickering, forever out of reach.

"Are you using those needles?" Brennan asked.

His voice dragged me back to class, and I shook my head,

handing the needles over. There were only six of us in Metal-work and Jewelry, and it was obvious everybody else wanted to be there.

They swirled their fingers through bowls of lamp-work beads, choosing another color, caring what came next on their wire.

When they twisted their pliers, their base wires became luxurious shapes, half-moons or Greek squares. They managed to suspend cheap seed pearls in loops and whorls. When they clamped off the clasps, no ragged edges remained.

Mrs. Baxter had demonstrated all of that in the first week. Mechanical technique she called it. I didn't have it.

Give me sink rope or claw bands. Give me zip ties and bait bags. I knew what to do with those. I could drop a lobster pot like it was a French-hook earring; it was elegant, even. But with delicate little pretty things, I was hopeless.

Don't get me wrong, I liked wearing it just fine. For my last birthday, Seth gave me a pair of silver wraps that held on to the top of either ear. I wore those almost every day, just like the silver stud in the curve of my nose.

I couldn't do rings or necklaces or anything that dangled—too easy to rip off when I was working the boat. But what I *could* wear, I liked. I just wasn't artistic when it came to making it.

And it's not like I didn't know that. I was supposed to have Forensics during third period. The school was so small, we had only two electives a semester. Solving fake crimes with the double-duty science teacher sounded like more fun to me than beading necklaces.

I don't know who changed my schedule. Could have been the principal (also, the dean and guidance counselor). Or my parents. I guess they decided that after Levi died, the last thing I needed was twelve weeks of dead bodies and the torment people put them through.

They were protecting me. And maybe they were right. At least Mrs. Baxter didn't expect me to be good at beading. I had a solid C for turning everything in on time, and she never asked me to explain my vision on critique days.

The class turned out to be soothing, in a way. We were allowed to talk, but we didn't much. It was all soft patter, *pass me that knotter,* and *could I have that clamp?* It sounded like distant rain, so many beads being poured from tray to tray, slipping easily on wires. They whispered, and so did we.

When Bailey opened the door, it disturbed the rain. We all looked up at the same time.

"From the office," Bailey said, and crept to my table. She touched the coiled mess of my project and said "pretty" before getting to the point. Smoothing a note onto the table, she told me what it said. "Your mom tried to text you, but you didn't answer."

"What's wrong?" I asked. I took a quick look at my phone, but it was blank. No big surprise. There was only one cell tower and nothing but rock and cliff for miles. We were lucky when we got a signal at all.

Bailey fished through the beads, pulling out a red and purple one to roll between her fingers. It would disappear into her pocket any time now; those were Cait's favorite colors. "You have to go home straight after. The lawyer's coming."

Not my lawyer, the prosecutor. I didn't bother to correct her. Instead, I brushed her hand away so I could pretend to work on my bracelet. Staring down at the silver loops, I said, "All right."

"Do you want me to come?" she asked.

Did I? Not really. "You can."

Rubbing her shoulder against mine, Bailey reached for another bead. "I'll do community service with you."

"Good," I said, frowning when my sight wavered, hot with tears. "'Cause I'll probably need a ride."

"I'm not getting my brakes fixed for you, princess. Just so you know."

"Who asked you to?"

She flipped me off behind Mrs. Baxter's back, and left. I was glad she hadn't looked too close. If I could get a couple breaths in, I could seal myself up. I wouldn't break down in the middle of class. They already knew I was guilty and nobody blamed me, anyway.

So what was there to cry about?

TWO

Grey

Sailors used to mark the edges of their maps **Here There Be Monsters**.

They weren't entirely wrong. Monsters don't have claws, they have eyes dark as molasses and hair white as a new dime. They have soft petal lips that whisper the sweetest promises.

I can say with absolute authority that one doesn't notice a cloak of fog if one is too entirely entranced with the creature wearing it.

It's the thing beneath, the thing you cannot imagine, that captures you.

Susannah had delicate fingers; she liked to pull them through my hair. I would close my eyes and exist under her hand. My heart beat for her touch. My blood ran for a single flash of her lashes. Not once did I question the mist at her feet. It seemed ethereal at the time.

My father's boat was fast; he had a talent for cutting ice. We sailed up the shore from Boston thrice weekly, buying lobster today to sell tomorrow while the beasts still waved their claws and curled their tails.

It was an idiotic profession. One he intended to press on me when I was of age to captain my own ship. He assumed I wanted it. That I would be no happier than at the moment I reflected him completely. But I stood on the deck of his ship and loathed him.

The man was gentle enough—many found him convivial company indeed. But I detested the cream he rubbed into his hands. As if any tincture might soften them and let him pretend to be a gentleman. I'd always wondered if he realized he stank of lobster. Even after a boiling bath with flowers and fresh soap: then he smelled of lavender and lobsters. It was no improvement.

I had bigger plans for myself. A life of adventure, one lived on rails and on horseback. Through cities and deserts. Oh, especially deserts—I fantasized about them. To bask in the heat all day long, to warm my feet in the sand. To spend not a single moment soaked with salt water. Whatever the hook that bound my father with the sea, I didn't possess it. And I had my plans to abandon it eternally.

Working the lobster line with my father offered me little entertainment, so I had to make me own. The island in the Broken Tooth harbor, that fascinated me. The villagers said it was abandoned, dangerous, haunted.

When my father and I sailed in, I studied its forbidding shape, wondered about its secrets. On our departure, I did the same, gazing and gazing at Jackson's Rock.

And it was in such contemplation that I saw Susannah for the first time. She stood on the island cliff in the bay, her hair unfurled, long locks tossed by the wind. With a pale cloak and gown, she seemed made of the mist.

Leaning over the side, I stared at her—I wondered earnestly if this was a siren. If she would open her mouth and sing. If she would draw our ship into the rocks beneath her feet.

Instead, she waved.

Her fingers bloomed like a peony bud, and there was a weight to her smile that I longed to lighten. She shrank as we slipped away on good winds. Soon she was nothing but a star on the horizon, and then nothing at all but a memory.

My thoughts troubled me: Was she the lighthouse keeper's daughter? Was she there alone? It was the shape of her smile that drew me back. In my ship's bunk, and in my bed at home, I invented in that expression a damsel that only I could rescue.

Certainly, her father had locked her away from the mainland; undoubtedly, her stepmother had made her a servant. She was a nymph or a princess, Snow White or Cinderella. She was Rapunzel, and in my fever, I felt certain that if I only asked, she would let down her platinum hair.

She did.

While my father attended to business in the village, I rowed to the rock. My shoulders burned, and the sun—so mild to just stand in it—spilled fire all across me. In dreams, I was dashing in my rescue, crisp in linens. In truth, I landed on the shore with my shirt soaked through and damp hair clinging to my face. The ocean. Always the godforsaken ocean.

"You shouldn't be here." Susannah stepped from the trees, a pale apparition.

Already lovesick from memory, the fresh sight of her only stoked the fever. Leaping ashore, I approached, hands out as if she might startle like a doe. I told her, "I came for you."

"Why?"

With every bit of foolish sincerity I had in me, I replied, "Because I love you."

In retrospect, I should have been surprised that she let me kiss her. That she threaded her fingers in my hair and whispered exactly the right words in my ear to entice me back. Our stolen moments were painted in romantic shades, in the bronze twilight beneath towering pines.

For an entire summer, again and again, I returned to her rock, to her pale and spectral kisses—until I swore I would do anything for her. I would die for her.

And then I did.

I was an idiot, and a fool, and I have had a century now to shame myself for mistaking lust for love. Every time I look in the mirror and see my dime-silver hair and my eyes dark as molasses—every time I look across the water to Broken Tooth, hoping that the girl thinking of me will soon come to my shore—I'm reminded of my stupidity.

And I hate myself only a little for hoping she's just as unwise.

THREE

Willa

I wasn't that late, but when I came in the back door, I was caked in mud and smelled like low tide.

Not a thing changed on Ms. Park's face when she saw me. With one of our chipped coffee cups in her hands, she looked over her case folders and said, "I'm glad you could make it."

She wasn't even sarcastic about it, but my mom raised an eyebrow anyway.

"Sorry. I was working."

"Bailey was here," Mom said.

Guilty, I dumped my gear on the porch and went straight for the sink. I needed a shower, but it could wait. I turned the water on hot and then flipped the switch for the garbage disposal. "I'll see her tomorrow."

Gargling furiously, the disposal swallowed sand and silt as I pretended not to notice the prosecutor. Only, I knew the longer I looked away, the longer she'd be there. Waiting. Head down, I asked, maybe not even loud enough to be heard, "What do you want, anyway?"

Ms. Park cleared her throat, then twisted her chair around. Its wooden legs screeled against the linoleum, and I felt her move closer. "We need to go over your grand jury testimony."

Digging mud from beneath my blunt nails, I said, "Don't you have what I told the police?"

"Of course I do," she replied. She sounded smooth, creamy even. The chair squeaked again, and then I could see her from the corner of my eye. "But I can't have any surprises when you're on the stand. You're the only eyewitness we have, Willa."

My tongue felt like liver, thick and heavy and useless. Everything I knew about courts and stuff came off TV, and it so happens that none of those shows get it right.

It's not neat and clean, talking to the detectives, then going to trial, the end. No, I talked to the Coast Guard and Marine Patrol and then the police the night Levi died. And the next day, a detective totted up in a suit came and took notes.

When they arrested Terry Coyne, I talked to the detective again. My dad stood at my shoulder during the lineup. Even that wasn't the same as TV.

They gave me a book of mug shots, rows and rows filled up with forty-year-old men with the same beaky nose and chickeny

35

chin. It was scary, how much those pictures looked alike. I didn't know until way after that I picked the right guy.

Now it was going to a grand jury. They had to decide whether there was enough evidence to indict him—whether there was even gonna be a trial. All the police had were two bullet casings that matched a box they found in Coyne's trunk, and me. My eyes. What I saw. It was down to two bullets and my memory whether he'd ever stand trial for murdering my brother. If that wasn't enough, he'd go free.

Cold, hard knots formed in my chest. "All right, what should I say?"

Ms. Park brushed her smooth black hair behind one ear and insisted, "I'm not here to put words in your mouth."

"Then what do you want? I already told the police everything."

"Everything?" Ms. Park let that question hang a minute. Then she went on. "Because I'm going to ask you about the gear war. It's the only way this murder makes sense. And if you say nothing . . ."

"There wasn't a gear war," I said flatly.

"We know Mr. Coyne put his traps too close to yours. We know your father complained to the council about it."

I shrugged. This, this part was Broken Tooth business. Ms. Park could ask all around town. Nobody would say gear war, because there wasn't one. It was one lobsterman, me, taking care of business. Our waters were ours, our rules our own. Levi wouldn't have told. He wouldn't want me to either.

All we did was cut and dump. We went easy on Coyne. Last year, in Friendship, somebody sank *Lobstah Taxi* and *Fantaseas* in the middle of the night. Couple years before that, it was a scuttling in Owls Head and a shooting in Matinicus. You got up on a fisherman's waters and he had to retaliate.

One fisherman against another, that was personal. When a whole town did it, orchestrated and arranged—*that* was a gear war. So I said nothing, and cast my gaze past Ms. Park.

She went on, barely ruffled. Working the sarcasm, she said, "Then, *coincidentally,* Mr. Coyne *just happens* to find you and your brother *minding your own business* on the wharf at two in the morning. Right after he discovered somebody cut all his trap lines, there you are. But it's *not related.*"

"It wasn't a gear war," Mom snapped.

"Then what was it?" Ms. Park snapped back.

My mother thrust herself between us, reaching for the potato scrubber. She took it to my fingertips, rasping them mercilessly. She hadn't done that since I was little; I could clean up after fishing and worming just fine on my own.

Still, she soaped and scoured, her thin fingers pressing hard into my palm. "Where're you from, Ms. Park? Concord?"

Unamused, Ms. Park said, "Boston."

Mom scrubbed a little harder, hiding the ugly sound she made.

The one that called the prosecutor a Masshole, after Mom had tried to give her an out by asking if she was from New Hampshire.

Back stiff and voice steely, Mom pulled my hands under the tap and said, "A gear war's something we'd vote on, in the village. It'd be all of us doing it, not just one kid, one night."

"Ma!"

Snapping her head up, she looked at both of us hard. "I'm not gonna let that bastard get off scot-free because *she* doesn't understand how things work here." Turning her attention to Ms. Park, she went on. "If you say 'gear war,' nobody on that jury's gonna listen to you."

"Then somebody needs to tell me what actually happened."

My head felt full; my ears ached, like I'd slipped too far under water. It wasn't a crime anymore to cut off somebody's gear, but I could lose my license for it. Three years before I could get it back. Three years when Daddy would have to pay a sternman to work the deck; all that time with money running out instead of flowing in.

I could fight it. Claim I didn't know anything about the cut gear. I could ask for a civil jury to decide it. If they found me liable, I'd have nothing. My family would have nothing.

Though I could keep worm digging, it wouldn't be enough. And the thought of watching the rest of the fleet sail without me, the prospect of standing on land instead of waves — that felt like dying.

But all that was *if* they found me liable. They probably wouldn't. Juries were *our* people. They understood you had to protect your waters. Turning their eyes the other way, they'd shake their heads. Shrug. They'd probably let me off. Probably, probably.

Could they, if I got in front of the grand jury and admitted it? I didn't know. Would Coyne get indicted if I didn't? I didn't know that either. My chest got tighter as I tried to balance the right thing with the way things were supposed to be.

Expectant, Ms. Park said, "Well?"

When I looked past her, I saw Dad sitting in his truck on the street. Orange light suddenly illuminated him. He was smoking again. Drawing on the cigarette, he sat back in the glow of the embers. He'd quit for Levi. That he was back on them, guess he thought we were already lost. Nothing was balanced, and I broke.

"I did it, all right?" I faced Ms. Park, clutching the edge of the sink behind me. "He kept dropping his gear on ours, and nobody'd do anything about it. He's not even from here. What's he doing fishing our waters?"

Ms. Park opened one of her folders. "Start at the beginning."

"You already got the beginning," I said.

I closed my eyes and listened to the sea in my memories. That night was so clear, I felt it on my skin. Cool wind and hot blood and the way my world ended in slow motion.

I didn't know it was ending, not at first. My laughter echoed across the deck of the *Jenn-a-Lo*, a little eerie and removed. A few minutes before, the night was bright and clear—a black sky spattered with stars, hung with a fat, silver moon.

But pearly silk fog suddenly blotted out the sky, the shore. I couldn't hardly see Levi in the wheelhouse, and he was three steps away. No one else could have seen us in the swirling haze, and that was good.

"How many are we going to do?" Levi asked. The question floated out to me, disembodied.

"All of them," I said.

I leaned on the rail. Dark waters stretched out all around me. They murmured against the side of the boat, sea whispers that lulled me to sleep at night and called me to fish in the morning. They taunted me when I was stuck in school. Better than anywhere in town, I could see the harbor from school.

One day, Daddy was gonna retire. I'd be captain then. And my kids or Levi's, they'd take up the stern. We'd been fishing in the shadow of Jackson's Rock for three hundred years. If I'd had my way, it woulda been three hundred more.

And that's why Levi and I snuck out in the middle of the night. It's why we stole the keys from Dad's pocket and slipped away from the wharf without a word to anybody.

Wielding the long, hooked gaff, I waited for the *Jenn-a-Lo* to glide up to the next green and blue buoy. I snagged it with the hook, and with a quick twist, I pulled it into the boat.

I wrapped the buoy end of the rope into the block, then wound it into the hauler. The whole time, I hummed the same note the hydraulics did, and watched as the lobster pot rose to the surface. Two fat lobsters waved their claws from behind wire mesh.

Sea spray stung my face; when I breathed, I tasted salt water and southwestern wind, and it was delicious. Trading the gaff for my knife, I cut the line between the buoy and the trap, then threw everything back in the water.

The lobsters would slip free on their own, but the traps would be lost, and that was the point. That's what this bastard from Daggett's Walk got for dropping trawls in Broken Tooth waters.

As the pot disappeared beneath the waves, I punched the air, burning on adrenaline. "Try hauling that!" I shouted.

Levi sped the engine and said, fondly, "Shut it."

"Your face!"

With that, Levi laughed too. "I refuse to upgrade to 'your mama's face.'"

"No wonder you're her favorite." I grabbed the gaff and leaned over the side again. The *Jenn-a-Lo* cut through the night, steady and sure, toward the next pair of pots.

It should have been *hard* to locate every line dropped by

another lobsterman. After all, part of the captain's job was plotting his own lines into the GPS so he could find them again later. And part of legacy fishing was having your own waters. Your own secret places, where nobody fished but you.

But the interloper had found every red-striped Dixon buoy and dropped his gear right next to them.

The first time it happened, Dad was willing to call it an accident. Piss-poor fishing by a piss-poor fisherman, he figured.

We dragged his traps away from ours. That knotted up his traps underwater and left him a mess to clean up. It should have sent a message. And since we had plenty of water left in the season, we moved our traps closer to Jackson's Rock.

Not two days later, green and blue buoys bloomed beside our trawls again.

This guy wasn't just sneaking into waters that didn't belong to him. He was outright stealing our catch and something had to be done.

Dad asked around and finally figured out it was Jackie Ouelette's cousin doing it. Carrying a six-pack and his calm, Daddy went up the hill to Jackie's place to talk to her about it.

Terry Coyne was there, and instead of talking, they had words. Coyne mentioned he was a boxer; Daddy pointed out he had a shotgun. Jackie got between them and sent my dad on home.

Not surprisingly, that little talk didn't fix anything. The next time Coyne's traps showed up on ours, Dad reported it to the Zone Council. He made sure everybody at the co-op knew where Coyne's lobster was coming from. They refused to buy his catch, but other than that?

Nothing.

Nothing happened, nothing stopped him. It added an extra hour to his day to sail to the next co-op, and they didn't give a damn where the lobster came from. Back in Broken Tooth, we were hurting, and nobody wanted to do anything about it.

So I bribed Levi to pilot the boat while I cut the lines on Coyne's gear. Levi would have been happier at home drawing manga or sitting on the roof with Seth and Nick, talking about anime. He went along because I was his big sister. Because I asked him to. Because he liked being out at all hours of the night.

But for me, it was payback, straight up. If nobody wanted to help, I'd help myself.

The ocean agreed with me; the sea was on my side. It was smooth as glass that night. The fog wrapped around me; it felt like a kiss. Pulling twenty of Terry Coyne's traps, I cut off every one and laughed the whole way.

Levi and I slid up to our slip at the wharf, still smiling. Me more than him, but it was one of those things. The thrill of getting away with something *together.* He hopped off the deck first and held his hand out for mine.

It never crossed my mind that Coyne might be out on the water too. He must have cut his engine the same time we did, so we didn't hear him approach.

"Hey, Dixon," he shouted.

We both turned, just in time for Coyne to appear in the mist. Just in time to see the gun, but not fast enough to do anything about it.

He fired twice.

It sounded like a wire snapping, hollow and high-pitched. It echoed forever, ebbing into the distance. I understood what happened, but I didn't *know* it. Not until Levi stumbled back onto the boat and fell into me.

Black blood spread on the front of Levi's shirt. And then it started spitting. His air poured out through his chest instead of his throat. My body moved on its own because I wasn't thinking.

Silence swallowed me. I snapped the tab on our EPIRB, our emergency beacon. The radio inside it crackled to life, sending a mayday to the Coast Guard. And because we were supposed to use it out at sea, a strobe burst to life on top of it.

Blinded, I sank to the deck and clapped a hand over the hole in Levi's chest. Heat spilled from it. Dark foam bubbled between my fingers. In my shock, I thought I saw his soul slipping out, a grey ghost that lingered near his chest.

But it was cold that night. It was just frost forming on the heat of his blood, the same way my breath hung in the air. Above us, the rescue beacon pulsed, lightning that bounced off the fog in eerie patterns.

"Coast Guard's coming," I told Levi.

The last thing Levi ever said was, "'Kay."

I kept thinking, *Too bad Dad doesn't smoke anymore,* because every time he watched *Platoon,* he'd tell us that the plastic wrap on a pack of cigs could close up a bullet hole. Slap it on, good as new. It was stupid trivia. Who even knew if it was true?

But that's what I was thinking while I tried to hold in my brother's last breath.

It wasn't until Ms. Park left that Dad finally came in. While I boiled mud and memories from my skin in the upstairs shower, I listened to him talk to my mother in the kitchen.

Not his words—I couldn't really pick them out. Just his voice, rising and falling. Slipping beneath my mother's voice, strange and dark. Maybe it was about me. I didn't know; I couldn't tell. But it felt like an accusation.

It was always obvious to my parents what happened that night. Pretty much the whole village knew and understood. Our waters were our waters. If Coyne hadn't dropped gear on top of ours, he'd have been dropping it on someone else's.

Broken Tooth didn't have much. We were all starving a little bit, shrinking every year. Bailey wouldn't come back. A degree in political science wouldn't do her any good around here. The bright ones like her, they went off to the world. To New York Cities and LAs and Londons. None of the Baileys came back.

Instead, tourists moved in, all romantic about living Down East. Untouched wilderness, rustic everything. Then they paved it and blocked off our beaches. They pitched a fit about how much noise we made in the harbor when we went out to fish. They held condo meetings about the stink of salted herring that lingered when we sailed out.

But our harbor was what we had. Our families and our town. The burying ground was full of slate gravestones, our names all the way back to the 1600s. Washburns, Dyers, Dixons. Archambaults and Ouelettes, on and on, over and over.

What I did, my neighbors woulda done too. The Coynes and the out-of-towners carried poison with them. No one in Broken Tooth would have blamed me.

Ducking my head under the water, I let heat flow through my hair and run the trail of my lips. Fresh water always smelled like blood, especially when it was turned up hot. The steam robbed me of deep breaths. I stared as sand collected in the bottom of the tub, slinking toward the drain.

Downstairs, Dad raised his voice, then the back door slammed. I didn't hear it so much as feel it, an unexpected slap.

Twisting the tap off, I listened to the silence that followed, then the low hum of his truck driving away.

They'd always known what I did, but tonight they had to admit it. The space gouged out of this house, this family, it was—

I was never afraid I'd get in trouble for cutting off Coyne's gear. It was the *telling* that scared me. The confessing. Having to look at my mother and my father afterward. Having to look at myself. Having to say it out loud:

It was my fault Levi was dead.

Not in some roundabout, butterflies-in-Africa-starting-hurricanes-in-Maine kind of way. My little brother would have been a Bailey. He had a soft smile, and notebooks full of art. Full of good song lyrics that Nick and Seth put to bad music. He made stop-motion movies, and flipbooks, and plans to give up the sea entirely.

He could've; he would have.

Except I leaned in his doorway that night. I waited for him to pull out his ear buds and ask me, "What up, Willard?"

And instead of saying "Let's go find the Grey Man" or "Nothing, I just wanted you to know I ate the last of your Trix on purpose," I tossed him the keys to the *Jenn-a-Lo*.

He caught them on the first throw.

THREE

Grey

There she is again, thinking about me.

I transfer my calipers to my left hand and peer at the music box on my desk. The coils are tightened, the clockworks pinned. Nothing rattles when I lift it to my face.

Turning the copper key, I hold it—master of time, the god of the figures trembling on top of the box. If they dance, it's because I wish it. If they hang forever in anticipation, that, too, is within my grasp.

But I let the key go, and it slowly unwinds. The "Maple Leaf Rag" is more a waltz at this pace. The figures circle each other, their copper skin glinting with each mechanical turn. Placing it in the window, I watch them sway against the line of the horizon. Tonight's sunset is red and bright—sailor's delight.

And mine, too, for she's thinking of me. She must be realizing, as I once did, that something lives on this rock. Tomorrow I shall stand on the cliff and wait. I will be the pale star that blinks on the horizon. I will be ethereal and tempting.

If there is any balance in the world, any justice between the heavens and the earth, she'll see me. Is that not the true nature of this curse? I've no chance of collecting a thousand souls. Nor did Susannah, nor any other Grey to stand on this island. The only escape is through another. A willful, if stupid, choice—she must say yes. She must choose this mantle.

I do believe she'll come. I could wish for it, for her to appear at my breakfast table the same way my books and toys and oddments do. But the bindings of the curse are clear: anything that I want will be mine.

Only by happenstance and the slightest shift of fog can I get what I need.

Tomorrow I'll hold back the mist, arrange myself handsomely. The wind will finger through my hair while I stand and wait. If there's any justice at all, I'll meet her eyes across the water and become her fascination.

Already she's thinking of me.

Now I just need her to come.

FOUR

Willa

"I could take Latin next year," Bailey said, "but I'd have to drop welding so I can drive all the way up to Herrington."

My head hurt. And much as I loved Bailey, I didn't know if I could go another two hours dissecting her senior year schedule. Since I wasn't going to college, I planned to take the five classes I needed to graduate. That would let me get out at one, so I could go pull traps with my dad. Well, that's what it used to be. I figured I'd be getting out at one to go pull bloodworms now.

That's what I was doing—sorting them at the cellar, anyway. The room was too cold and stank of fish and mud. The professional worm diggers, the ones who made their whole living year round on it, had already gone. They counted faster than we did. And maybe they didn't want to hear about dead languages versus vocational arts either.

Bailey was overachieving like usual. She already had three years of Spanish. She didn't *need* Latin. Not like she needed welding, because her truck was about to fall apart. It was probably two sticks of gum and some duct tape away from collapsing into parts.

One more language on her transcript would look good. And she was gonna twist her schedule until she got it. I already knew the ending, so it was hard to get excited about the journey.

After a while, she noticed I was only offering her *uh huh*s and *yep*s. Her plastic sorting tray thumped against mine. My pile of worms was smaller than hers. Probably because I'd been counting instead of talking.

"Are you listening?"

I had to shake my head. "Not really. Sorry."

Shifting her tray again, she started pulling the shorties to one side. We got paid less for those. She made a leap I hadn't. "I know you hate letting Seth go out with Dad. Somebody has to, though."

"I'm well aware."

"Quit being so damned old," she said.

"I'm not," I sniped back. "I've got a lot on my mind. I can't imagine *why.*"

This time, Bailey cracked her tray against mine on purpose. "You're allowed to be depressed. You're not allowed to feel sorry for yourself."

"And why not?"

Bailey had a fire going inside. Probably tindered when she was on time to talk to Ms. Park and I wasn't. She'd had a couple of days to feed it. While she was good enough not to play silent-treatment games on me, I sometimes wondered if I wouldn't have liked that better.

"Because you shut everybody out and make it worse. On purpose. Things won't get magically better because you punish yourself."

"Who said it would?"

Starting to clap a hand to her face, Bailey stopped at the last minute. She wasn't mad enough to rub worm all over her cheek. "You act like it, and you know it."

"So you say."

"So I know," she retorted.

Picking up my Styrofoam cup, I dumped the rest of my worms in it. Back stiff and jaw tight, I didn't look away. I wasn't afraid of Bailey. I knew her secrets, and she knew mine. Arguing with her was as safe as it got. In the morning, she'd still love me. Even if she was mad. Carrying my collection to the register, I turned back to her. And because I didn't have anything to say that was true, I flipped her off instead.

With a sneer, she put her head down to finish counting.

Mom worked second shift at police dispatch, and Dad fished from dawn 'til dusk. That meant whoever got home first made dinner.

It used to be Levi, and it was too bad it wasn't anymore. He could find three random things in the pantry and make a meal. I could follow instructions on a box, more or less.

Low tide came twice a day most days. I'd already earned a couple hundred at the noon low. I could hit the next at midnight, but Seth's flannel shirts, one I'd stolen from his bedroom, beckoned. It smelled like him. It felt like him wrapping his arms around me, my only constant.

Once I had it on, it was decided. I was done worm digging.

I jogged downstairs to find something easy to make. Bacon and eggs would be plenty for me. But Seth and Dad would be starving when they came in, so I pulled a box of pancake mix from the pantry, butting it against the grease jar as I went back for jam and syrup. The phone rang before I managed to crack one egg.

"Don't worry," Mom said when I answered.

Tension laced me tight. Leaning against the counter, I turned the burners off one by one, pretty sure that whatever I wasn't supposed to worry about meant I wouldn't be home long enough to need hot pans. Somehow, I sounded calm when I asked, "What's going on?"

She cleared her throat, then I heard her talking to someone

else. Way to drive me crazy, to make sure that knot in my throat was as big as it could be. Finally, she came back and said, "I don't want you coming up here, Willa. I just wanted you to know your dad's up at the hospital with me, but he's all right."

A slow, sharp pain pierced my temple. "What happened?"

"He was gaffing a buoy and wouldn't let go. Got knocked on his ass."

It was a stupid mistake to make, getting hauled down the deck because he didn't want to lose a cheap hook—a greenhorn mistake. One that could pull you overboard, drown you before anyone realized you were gone.

Anger welled in my chest. He shouldn't have been on deck to begin with. That's why Seth was there. Pressing fingers to my brow, I tried to smooth away the ache. "What did he do that for?"

"Just an old fool, I guess." She said something I couldn't hear again, then went on. "We'll be home as soon as somebody tracks down the doctor, but don't wait for us."

"And tell her to stay off the boat," Dad said in the background.

For some reason, my mother didn't repeat that. Instead she said, "Your boy should be dropping by, so you know."

The crunch of gravel out front proved her right. I didn't have to turn to recognize the sound of Seth's truck in our driveway. But everything inside me felt curiously empty. I didn't move;

Seth would let himself in. All my friends did, and he was more than that now, wasn't he?

"Willa?"

Shaking my head, I pushed off the counter. "I think I hear him now. Tell Daddy he's on bait until he learns his lesson."

"I'll do that," she said, and hung up as the side door opened.

Filling the space, Seth looked wrecked. His face was drawn. Dismay darkened his eyes, which seemed nearly black against his ashen skin. The way he started toward me, it was a good thing Mom had called first. Just to look at him, I would have guessed somebody else had died.

Seth caught me in his arms, burying his face against my hair. "Baby, I'm sorry."

Slowly, I wrapped my arms around Seth's waist. "Mom says he's fine. I heard him complaining, so I know it's true."

"I'm sorry," he repeated. "Everything got tangled in the hauler, and . . ."

"It's all right." I spread my hands across his back, rubbing muscles stiff from work and worry. It felt like a chore at first. Something automatic like the lighthouse, the right motion for the moment. It kept me from thinking too much. From pointing out I'd warned him about the hauler.

By inches, Seth melted against me, and we ended up swaying. We were a slow pendulum, and listening to his reedy breath thawed some of my numb, cooled some of my anger. When he kissed my brow, my heart turned and I clung to him. The house would have been too quiet without him. My thoughts would have been too loud.

"You want me to stay?" he asked.

"Yeah, you can help with dinner."

And he did; he knew where everything was. He also knew a little cinnamon in the pancake mix made it special. I knew the syrup would explode in the microwave if we left the cap on. We were solid, and certain—a team.

The window framed us, night glass reflecting us—and for a moment, I stared. We fit exactly. Always had. Everyone knew it. Like the moon changed shape, like the sun came up—the two of us were meant to be. In third grade, Bailey and Amber chased me across the playground, throwing dandelion heads and singing:

Tikki-tikki-tembo, Seth Ar-sham-bow
Kissing Willa Dixon, in her mama's kitchen!
Gonna get married, gonna get married, boo!

They sang it until I cried, and Mrs. Graham sent them to time-out.

No idea why it upset me.

FOUR

Grey

Susannah wasn't the first girl I loved. Nor the third nor the sixth. I was entirely indiscriminate with my affections. The pretty girls were the only benefit to following my father from Massachusetts to Maine, from Boston to Nova Scotia.

All else was torment, but always on the shore, lovely girls. Girls with exotic accents. With brown eyes, blue, and green. With parasols and gowns that draped them as if they were Grecian goddesses. They distracted me from the hardships of merchant life. In return, I treated them from the stores.

Tea from Boston, mostly. It made a good gift—it wasn't expensive, it didn't spoil. I trailed spiced leaves all along the shore, filling cups wherever I walked.

In the beginning, the very beginning, I thought perhaps this lighthouse was my penance. That here, I would learn to be selfless. To become a man, someone worthy of esteem. I was by beauty trapped and thus made a beast. It made sense that by beauty I would be set free.

How brilliantly I deceived myself. But, in my own defense, isn't that the conclusion bred into us by the Misters Grimm and M. Perrault? (Hr. Anderson seemed rather more occupied with eternal suffering and thus wasn't a favorite of mine.)

I offered pretty prayers. I wished for a rosary and learned it. Then mala beads, then bells. I wished for a singing bowl and tried rather hard to learn to meditate. But I had nothing but the sea to surround me. Its whisper, constantly in my ears. I was the most shut away of monks, but I never found pleasure in it.

Always my downfall. Pleasure, the wanting of it. The pursuit of it. I ignored my true calling for a decade. Though I held the mists off, I thought, This is my test. If I suffer it nobly, I'll be rewarded. Another girl will come, I'll be transformed. I've learned my lesson and stopped hating the ocean.

These are lies. Sometimes I repeat them. It makes the hours, one after the other, same as the last, same as the next, go by. And now, my reward is at hand. My release. My freedom, and though in those early days I swore I would be better, I swore I would never press a cursed kiss on anyone the way Susannah had pressed one on me—

I realized, I had meant it only halfway. Because there, on the shore, she's thinking of me. If she'll only come, I'll press this curse on her without hesitation. I'll do it with the truth. With revelation. She'll see every sweet benefit, and it's no concern to me if she discovers the disadvantages. By then, it will be much too late.

And besides. She'll need that discovery to fuel the first ten years. After that, she'll manage on her own.

FIVE

Willa

The next day, Seth waited for me on the main stairs.

Light filtered through the stained-glass window on the upper landing, blues and greens and golds that wavered like water. The colors played through Seth's hair and reflected on his skin. He was built too rough and angular to call beautiful, but there was a reason girls craned out their car windows to get a look at him when we went to Bangor.

His smile bloomed when he saw me. Dumping his cracked paperback into his satchel, he hooked an arm around my waist and greeted me with a kiss. He pulled back, brushing his rough lips against my temple, and asked, "How's Dad?"

"Feeling like a dumbass," I said. "He says he wants to go back out as soon as he can."

Without hesitation, he nodded. "I can miss school, no problem."

He was so earnest. So damned earnest, thinking he was helping me. Like I was avoiding the boat on purpose. "I don't want him to go out. How did he even get hurt last time? He wasn't paying attention, and that's dangerous."

"I know, Willa. But he can't stay ashore forever," Seth said.

"Well, yeah."

With another kiss against my temple, he said, "I could get Nick to pull the traps with me so Dad wouldn't have to go."

That was Seth's best friend, a lumbering, shaggy guy who practically lived at Seth's house. I liked Nick; everybody did. But his family was from Indiana, and he'd be hard-pressed to tell the difference between a lobster trap and a beehive.

So I was nastier than I meant to be when I asked, "Oh yeah? Does Nick even have a license?"

"It's for one day."

"That makes a big difference to the Marine Patrol."

He stiffened a little, his hand going cold and heavy on my shoulder. Ducking beneath his arm, I walked a few steps ahead. I was afraid he'd spill into the hollow inside me. His hurt wouldn't fill me up; it would drown me. "It's all right. I'm gonna cut out for the flats; tell Bailey, all right?"

"You need a ride?"

His expression smoothed; watered light rippled across his face. A streak of green illuminated his eyes, then danced away to leave them dark. He meant it when he offered to drive me, but I shook my head anyway. I just wanted to get away, from him, from myself, I didn't even know. From my life in all the after.

Seth lowered his voice. "I'm here, Willa."

It should have made me happy that he could read me. That he knew me like that. But I didn't want to give him credit for growing up with me. For being good; for being the one who knew where we were supposed to be going. It was easy to be angry with him, *at* him.

I said, "I'm fine. Tell Bailey."

A couple of people wound past us, an embarrassing reminder that we weren't having this nothing fight someplace dramatic and quiet. I guess it was good that people like us didn't have to scream. Seth pressed his lips together, then waved a hand toward the door. The gesture said he'd tell Bailey; it invited me to go.

"Don't you let Nick on my boat," I replied, and let myself outside.

People talk about crisp autumn days, and maybe if I'd hiked into the woods, I might have enjoyed one. The colors had started to come in, copper ornament between firs and pines. Worn paths revealed bare stone beneath the soil and seeds, smooth from centuries of hikers.

But it wasn't the woods for me. I walked home in a damp, clasping cold to get my worming gear. Then I followed the shore to one of the inlet flats.

The fog had thinned, but in places it lingered. It snaked across the grey mud, stirring around my ankles.

Late for low tide, I had to slog almost to the water to claim an untouched spot. The air smelled like fish and seaweed and the bloody waft of new-turned mud. I had my rake in hand, but instead of bending to get to work, I turned to consider Jackson's Rock.

It looked like a cairn: a pile of granite boulders weathered to orange, capped with a thick head of jack pines. Mostly, it wore dark evergreens. Right at the point, though, a single, skeletal hemlock kept watch over the water.

Jutting above that, a sturdy, plaster white column cut the sky —our lighthouse. Even in daylight, it flashed a red light every nine seconds, calling souls and sailors home.

But there was no one there. The foghorn moaned when a computer told it to. The light pulsed by remote control. And my head ached when I tried to picture the east side of the island, the only place the cliffs collapsed to a shore. It was like Jackson's Rock wanted to be forgotten.

I bent over to get to work, raking mud, wrestling worms into my bucket before they bit or escaped. My rake gasped through the mire, and the cold became a constant. Its own ache, one that usually scrubbed away thoughts and worries. But today, the lighthouse distracted me.

No, it was the fog.

Maybe it was both. They'd always been there, and I never thought about them. It woulda been like thinking about my own hip, or my middle toe. Some things were just *there*. Some things just *were*.

Still, it seemed to me like I knew a hundred reasons why nobody went to Jackson's Rock. No shoreline to land on. Couldn't get a boat past the shoals anyway. It was a nature preserve for nesting peregrines. It was infested with bats; it was dangerous to breathe all their dried crap. It was haunted. It was dangerous. There was nobody in the lighthouse. There was *nobody* in the lighthouse.

A fine wire of pain pierced through my head, but it didn't stop me from thinking it. From feeling it. Maybe knowing it:

There was *somebody* in the lighthouse.

Cloudless skies came with morning and brought a sea barely rippled by the wind. I ate breakfast alone and dressed for school. Every time I caught a look outside, I hesitated. Our sugar maple had turned, half scarlet, half gold, and it seemed to sparkle in the pure light.

A transparent sunrise promised good weather all day, and I groaned when I stepped onto our porch. It was just cool enough to taste clean. No freeze in the wind to sneak into open collars or down the front of spray-soaked oil clothes.

The quiet pressed around me. Our fleet was nothing but shadows on the horizon, all set sail before first light.

I turned away. I had school. I told myself that like I really cared about it. Like it should grieve me to miss it.

Making my way toward the overlook hill, I felt the *Jenn-a-Lo* behind me. She didn't care that I was banned from her deck. She needed the sea; she wanted to cut across the waves to our fishing grounds.

Halfway up the hill to school, I looked back. All along the asphalt roads, a twine of roofs made up our town. Strung like Christmas lights, they draped city limits from one end to the other. Pines swayed between them, and a white steeple signaled due east.

Just then, some of the little kids from town ran past. They held hands, a bright, giggling wall that swept me from the path. I stood in the soft, fallen needles, my back to the school. From that vantage, everything looked sharper, Broken Tooth revealed.

And I was right. The harbor *was* empty, mostly empty—the

Jenn-a-Lo remained. She pulled at her slip, untouched and un-worked. Beyond her, terns circled Jackson's Rock, an endangered halo drawing attention to the lighthouse.

Something (some*one*) drifted across the island's cliffwalk. A hook drew through my belly. I shielded my eyes to get a better look at the thing on the island. It glinted, like a piece of glass catching the sun. Drifting through the trees, it flashed once more, then faded.

There were reasonable explanations. Maybe somebody from the Coast Guard was out there, checking on the beacon. Could be Fisheries and Wildlife counting active nests and live birds.

Before I could puzzle it out, Denny Ouelette veered toward me. "What are you staring at, dummy?"

My throat snapped closed. Denny was related to Terry Coyne, by marriage, not blood. Still, standing that close to her made my nerves fire. Lawyers had told me not to talk about the case; common sense agreed. Better to keep my mouth shut. Things were tense enough.

"My gran has to sell her house on account of you," Denny said. She was shorter than me, and made out of delicate parts. Tiny hands, doll mouth—she looked breakable. But we'd grown up together, and I knew better.

Out of reflex, and sincere, I said, "I'm sorry."

Like a snake, Denny coiled. Her eyes narrowed, and I could

see her calculating. Could she break my nose with one shot? Had I sounded snotty enough for her to get away with it?

Adrenaline buzzed through me; in a sick way, it almost felt like happiness. Already, I could taste blood; I savored the anticipation of the blow.

Her sums must have come up short, because the blow never came. Instead, she spat on the ground—near my shoes, but not on them. Then she pulled her hair from her coat and stalked up the hill to first class. Her perfume, sugar and light, lingered even after she disappeared inside.

My anticipation turned sour, and an ache started in my head. Somewhere on the top of the hill, Bailey waited for me. Seth, too. I could tell them about Denny. I could tell them anything. Then they'd stand too close and be too good.

A cool breeze threaded through my hair, bringing in the sea, washing it over me. I took one more step toward school, giving my feet the chance to make me behave. But they turned instead. Toward the harbor, toward Daddy's boat and the ocean.

But I'm the one who took the step.

It was a perfect day to be on the water, and there was only so much perfect to go around. I was desperate to go out, the sun bleaching my hair brighter and the wind chapping my lips. I wanted back all the things I'd lost, all the things that had slipped away.

I *wanted;* it wormed through me. It writhed under my skin.

It didn't take long to walk to the harbor. Gliding over the warped wood of the dock, I felt my blood surge again. I was heat, inside and out. Herring gulls pierced the sky with their bodies and their cries. Jumping on deck, I didn't bother to pull on my life vest. I went straight to the wheel; I steered straight out to sea.

As soon as I got past Jackson's Rock, I planned to throttle down and check the GPS. We had traps out; they needed to be pulled. It was a lot slower to run a lobster boat alone. Some people thought more dangerous, but it was possible.

To hell with black, biting worms and slinking around on dry land. To hell with bad-luck ladies onboard . . . I couldn't bring myself to cuss Daddy, but he had it coming for banning me from the boat. He knew how to hurt me because we were the same. I was his reflection; we were made of salt and sea and legacy, both of us.

As I left shore behind, the color came back to my world. I breathed again. My eyes opened. Then I cursed under my breath.

There are phantoms on the ocean. Ships sailed by the unseen; fae women and horses running beneath the waves. Mermaids and sirens, and all kinds of monsters—generations of sailors have seen them all.

That's why I cussed instead of gasped. Because that morning when I went back to sea, I looked past the waves to the mist-shrouded cliffs.

And from them, the Grey Man looked back.

FIVE

Grey

My celebration is simple. I raise my hands, and every music box plays at once.

To other ears, it might be cacophony. Minor keys sob while major keys elate, none of the times deign to match. Each coil runs its own length—some songs ending after a phrase. Others linger, gold notes that swirl in the air around me like dust motes.

In the end, just one tune remains. An old Irish song, and I knew all the words once. I forget them now.

One of my father's men liked to play it when we sailed home to Boston. He stood in the crow's-nest with a pipe and played the ballad into the wind.

Of the lyrics, I remember a single line: "It will not be long, love . . ."

Oh, promises. Promises! She looks to the island, and she sees me here. Though I've wanted it, longed for it . . . been so achingly aware of it, this is the moment when she's real. The moment that's the same for her: when I become real to her, too.

Laughter rolling through me, I raise my hands again. I turn in the gallery, and every music box sings. Again, again, again!

SIX

Willa

Bailey put the thought in my head. That's what I told myself, putting my stern to the Rock.

A thin finger stirred in my brain, making my head ache. The pain pulsed along with the engine. It got worse when I tried to pin down what I'd seen.

A bright streak for the black eyes, a low, thrumming thunder for the full curve of the lips. It was a strange, beautiful face, haloed by silver hair, cloaked in fog. Thinking about it made my head hurt so bad, my stomach turned.

I'd never been seasick, and I wasn't gonna start. Playing back the plots in the GPS, I turned the *Jenn-a-Lo* to our waters. It wasn't long before I came up on our first buoy. Throttling the engine, I stepped on deck and reached for the gaff. As I leaned to pull the first trap, I hesitated.

It felt like somebody was watching me. Turning slowly, I looked at the open sea all around. The day was too clear, too perfect, to be hiding anyone. The Marine Patrol and the Coast Guard never tried too hard to hide. What was the point? By the time they caught you doing something, it's not like you had any-where to run.

"Knock it off and fish," I told myself.

Hooking the first trawl, I dragged the wet line into the hauler and switched it on. A trap rose to the surface in a sparkling ring of bubbles. A skinny lobster clicked at me, lazy and halfhearted. Maybe it felt like it had to put on a show.

Pulling it free, I turned it over. Deep, dark green against my orange Kevlar gloves, it waved its swimmerets in surrender. No eggs clustered beneath the tail, no notch to mark it a breeding female either. The beast spanned the length of my metal ruler and then some. A keeper.

I tossed it into the live tank and scooped new bait into the bag. Tied that in the trap, then checked my position. Careful to cover my tracks, I dropped the trap exactly where Daddy had. He'd never know I was on the water.

The school might call, but I'd missed plenty of days onshore. The rest of the fleet had followed the lobster out deep; I'd be out and back before they sailed in for the night. Best yet, there was no reason to question my money from the co-op. Lobster was richer than bloodworms, but I could parcel it out.

It was slow, hauling traps alone. Stopping at every single buoy, pulling and emptying. Baiting and dropping it over the rail, only then moving to the next. It was slow, and it was hard.

But my shoulders didn't even burn. They sang. My whole body did, back to doing what it was made for. My clothes got wet, and my skin got gritty with salt, and it was heaven.

All around me, the ocean played. Waves kissed the side of the boat. Wind hummed strange melodies, and there were echoes on the water. Sounds I couldn't place or follow back. Sometimes it was a groan; sometimes a sigh. It was life, the water alive.

I felt sorry for the mainlanders, the people who thought lobster came from Plexiglas tanks. The people who thought sea salt was a gourmet name for the same stuff they poured out of blue boxes.

Those people didn't know what it was to stand on deck, surrounded by nothing but the elements. It felt complete; I felt holy —just me and the ocean that made up most of the world.

Before sunset, the sky darkened. A deeper shade of blue, it told me to turn back. Without a single cloud before me, I was tempted to go for one more. Maybe two more. Maybe finish the string.

But there were fishing hours, and I was in enough trouble. I needed to fill up again, on bait, on fuel. I needed to get my lobster to the co-op before they died. Fishing was complicated enough when you were *supposed* to be doing it. I had to be satisfied with ten traps, and a promise to do more soon.

I lied to myself a little when I plotted my way home. With the tide going out, the shoals on the west side of Jackson's Rock would be dangerous. I *had* to go around the east side. Wasn't my fault that's where the cliffs turned to beach. Had nothing to do with me that the Grey Man lived there.

The headache came back, sharp but strangely sweet. It was a dizzy kind of ache. Alluring, I guess. So when I sailed past Jackson's Rock, I slowed, but I didn't stop. It was enough to look at the shore, really look at it. Funny thing was, I'd sailed past it a thousand times, but I couldn't remember *seeing* it before.

It was a secret, the other side of that island. And I couldn't help but feel like I was the only one who knew it.

Daddy wasn't sleeping in the armchair in the living room, he was just pretending to. The cut over his brow wasn't much of anything. He held his arm like it should have been in a sling, though.

Pity mixed with annoyance, that's what I felt. He knew better than to hold on to the gaff, but he was still hurt, and he was my father.

And since he was acting, I decided to go along. Carefully, I closed the door, my fingers pressed to the edge to dull the sound. Then I stood on the inside welcome mat, still and holding my breath.

"Hm?" he mumbled, turning his head in my direction. Still pretending.

Pulling a wad of bills from my jeans pocket, I thumbed through them, then left half my cash in the ashtray Daddy used for his pocket change. I kept the rest for later. Then, as I headed for the stairs, I murmured, "It's just me."

"Mm-hm." He turned his face toward the window again. The hospital let him keep a pair of slippers, it looked like. That explained why his toes curled in pink, fuzzy footies. He'd been known to wear cranberry plaid, but there was no way he'd picked those out.

"I've got homework," I said.

"The school called."

My insides sank. Grabbing the banister, I turned back. "Yeah?"

"They're saying you've missed twelve days this year," he said. There was a strange note in his voice, and finally, he looked at me. "Where you been?"

"Worm digging, mostly."

Daddy and I weren't talking people. We could work together a whole season and say maybe three things. But there was a difference between quiet and silence, and ever since Levi died, what hung between me and Daddy was silence. It had weight; it made me feel ashamed.

Shifting from one foot to the other, I waited a minute, then decided he was done talking. Hauling myself up the stairs two at a time, I almost reached the landing before he called me back.

"Take your money."

"It's extra," I said.

"I don't care if it's fruit salad. It's yours, so you keep it." Daddy closed his eyes, back to a liar's sleep.

Acid rolled in my stomach, washing lazily from one side to the other. The mortgage was just about due; the utilities, too. We'd never discussed the bills, and definitely not me paying them. There was slack, and I'd picked it up. It's what we did; it was my house too.

Until then, nobody had questioned the money I left in the ashtray (though I think it was safe to say we all knew it wasn't from Santa).

I rubbed my hands together. "I'm trying to do my part."

His jaw tightened. It made the knot on his forehead stand up, showing off the cut there a little better. "You've done enough."

How many ways did he mean that? I couldn't tell, but it cut all the same. I stepped down but didn't let go of the rail. Instead, I let words out, daring to challenge his decision, and worse, his pride. "We're gonna need fuel oil this month. Mom says that's five hundred right there."

"Willa," he warned.

"Daddy," I replied.

"Don't make me raise my voice."

In flashes and strobes, I crossed the room. Then I was back on the stairs, shoving bills into my pockets. Everything between was a great blank. My head echoed with things I didn't say. Like, *Nobody makes you do anything, Daddy,* and *What's your freaking problem, anyway?* I didn't *like* worm digging. I didn't *want* to be the one paying the bills.

Storming upstairs, I wanted a hundred reckless, useless things at once. All the things I could have bought with my roll. A new cell phone, a box of Passion Flakies. Oreos and ice cream, and a bobblehead for Bailey's truck. Some useful things too. A laptop. A used boat and the tools to start fixing her up.

That last one felt like cheating on my family; shame chewed at me. But then Dad raised his voice. I don't think he was yelling at me. Just yelling, but I still heard him. It was still *about* me.

A newspaper flapped downstairs, and Dad shouted, "I can keep my own goddamned house."

"Who said you couldn't?" I yelled back.

"Shut up!"

My thin veneer of numb broke. Heat and emotion spilled together, and I caught the frame of the door to steady myself.

That man downstairs, that wasn't my father. That was Bill Dixon, who boxed bare-knuckle and wouldn't let you buy him a beer because he wanted whiskey instead.

The same Bill Dixon who'd decked his best friend to keep him from jumping into a winter sea; who took a punch from Mal Eldrich like it was a kiss. I'd never met that man. He'd been a legend, a ghost.

Right until then.

I closed my bedroom door and leaned against it. Not to cry, but to pack my heart away. Squeezing my feelings into beads, I pinned them together and let them roll out of sight. Let them stay in the dark, and be small, and easy to ignore. Then, like nothing happened, I peeled out of my salt-stiff clothes and checked my phone. Bailey'd texted around lunchtime, and I was just then getting it.

There's a party on Garland Beach, you coming?

Yeah. Yeah, I was.

SIX

Grey

The things I see from my brilliant prison.

A curse is a curse—the trappings are beautiful. They have to be, to tempt the eye, to sway the heart. The gilt packages, the plates that fill with any delicacy I like, they're the sugar in the poison. The way I look —the way Susannah looked—ethereal monsters. I'm a devil with an angel's smile.

The one that's been thinking of me—she saw me today. I barely saw her, but I stood on the cliff and I felt her come close. She hesitated; she saw through the magic for just a moment, and that moment was enough. I'm still imaginary to her, but I'm almost real. She had to disbelieve at first; I certainly did.

But I'm in her thoughts. And that's what matters.

If she's anything like me, if she's anything like the others in this chain of unfortunate souls, her thoughts will grow. She'll dream me, and wonder about me, and polish all her considerations until she has to come. Until she has to stand before me: to touch me, to know my face.

And my face is beautiful.

Her face is light. That's what they all are, out there. That's what I see when I watch this village, cursed but never realizing it.

When it's especially clear, and until lately, I've made sure it's always especially clear, I can see the houses. Ivory and cranberry and blueberry and brown—they dot the hills, a delectable harvest in every season. I see the churches and their proud steeples. I see doors opening. Windows closing.

But the people—they're no more substantial than the orchestra that plays in my music boxes.

They're points of light. In the day, only the brightest ones, the ones that sail past my lighthouse, are visible to me. But at night, oh. I don't look at the sky anymore; I watch the shore. All those souls are constellations that move.

Tonight, they've clustered together on the shore. A bonfire glows. It spits embers into the air. I'm imagining it, but I think I can smell the smoke. The sweet sea and a wood fire, all washed by the gathering mist.

I have nothing to do with it. If it comes, it comes. I'm done reining the elements for them. Instead, I watch them swirl across the beach. Jealously; I admit that. There are so many of them. They're a cloud of fireflies. The bright ones dazzle, but they don't interest me.

The dim ones make me ache. With my cursed eyes, I see only their lives, the length of them, the strength of them. If they're long for this world, they grow bright. Short for it, and they're much dimmer. There's a few on that beach who may as well be dead. Soon, they will be. I ask sweetly in my thoughts, Could you die on the water for me?

It doesn't matter if they drown. If they have influenza. If they come to blows, if they fire their guns, if some freak accident takes them — so long as they fall on the waves illuminated by my lighthouse.

My reach stretches twenty miles on every side but the landward one. At the stony shoreline, they're beyond my reach. So if they could slip into the water before they breathe their last, it would be lovely.

It's the least they could do for me.

I've been a good steward for this town; better than most. I've been honorable. They've had a hundred years of my generosity, holding back the fog. So many good days for them. So many clear days. I've been patient. In all this time, I could have blinded hundreds of fishermen. Led them astray, helped their pretty little boats crash into rocks, hidden coming storms.

Many would have; I understand now that Susannah drowned as many as she could before she realized that time and mathematics would betray her.

So I've been a true gentleman. I've cleared their skies. Not once in these hundred years have I killed anyone. I collected souls, but only those that came by accident and happenstance.

When I need it, there's a wall-length cupboard below the gallery. It's lined with glass jars.

Yes, in all my faery-tale certainty that I was meant to redeem myself on this island, I failed to acknowledge two things.

First, my dominion over the mists, and second, the jar cupboard. Ten years dragged on until a rowboat sank in the harbor. The jars chimed; they demanded my attention.

I uncapped one, and that soul all but collected itself. A hum filled the room, as if it were satisfied. And I, too, felt the faintest measure of peace. A taste of hope, a realization that I could free myself from this curse without any reflection on my character at all.

After all, the seas are voracious. Sailors and swimmers disappeared into them all the time. Except not so many as I thought. Not so readily. Until this summer past, I collected only two more souls. This summer, I finally raised that total to four.

Four in a hundred years. Rarely do I use my arithmetic anymore, but I can figure that sum.

Twenty thousand, four hundred, ninety-six years.

Longer than the course of all written human history. Longer than the memory of mankind itself. Thus, the anatomy of a perfect curse. It seemed possible. It hinted that I might keep my soul and morals yet. Simply let nature have nature's way and benefit from it.

But no—there aren't so many tragedies beneath my light as it might seem.

If I were to sharpen my teeth and learn to relish the prospect of drowning the innocent, I must be honest. There aren't enough of them in Broken Tooth. If I cull them all at once, their families will flee my shores. None would sail beneath my light.

Clever, clever curse. Twenty thousand, four hundred, ninety-six years.

It's been but a hundred, and I'm already sick of silence. Of magic. Of presents. Of kindness and generosity and honor and myself. Clutching the rail, I consider throwing myself over it. It's a childish thought, stupid drama for no audience at all, and worse, it won't make the slightest bit of difference.

The lamp grinds behind me, spinning ceaselessly. Its heat stings— I'm here, I feel it. But my body doesn't break its beam. I am insubstantial.

Those lights on the beach have no idea I'm watching them. Wanting them. Plotting against them. Ignorant, every one of them—they dance; they sway. They're just far enough away that I can't enjoy their music or eavesdrop on their conversations.

Right now, I hate them more than anything. And I'm glad, so glad, that she's thinking about me.

It didn't take long to change my mind. To do the things I swore I would never do. Just one hundred years—but what is that in the face of twenty thousand, four hundred, ninety-six?

SEVEN

Willa

The party got to me before I got to it. Music echoed down the beach, and people were laughing. Somebody threw another log on the bonfire, and a cloud of fire swirled toward the sky. Silver ash drifted over the water, disappearing into the dark.

Across the waves, Jackson's Rock loomed in fog and shadow. Couldn't even see the slender body of the lighthouse, just the beam as it swung over us. The pines were brushstrokes jutting from the mist; the cliffs seemed to rise from nothing.

When the foghorn sounded, its call rolled through the dark and the haze. Like it was alive; like it might draw me across that light bridge and into the secrets of the Rock. Harbor bells rang, like church bells on a wedding day.

I stood for a minute, staring like I'd never seen my own harbor before.

My head was so clear; I wasn't thinking about anything. Aware, yeah, of the six-pack dangling from my fingers, and the steamy scent of hot rocks and boiling water. But I was alone in myself for a minute. No guilt, or anger, or fear.

Then something glittered on the island cliff. My imagination rushed up to name it the Grey Man. Fantasy tried to fill in the shape I'd seen on Jackson's Rock—out there, fishing alone, and that reminded me. I *was* guilty. Afraid. Angry. That's all that put me on the beach. I gritted my teeth; going to this party was like going to war.

I was going to drink and laugh and dance. Burn my fingers on littleneck clams and steamed corn. If somebody wanted money for a grocery run, I had it. If Seth wanted to disappear into the caves with just us and a blanket, I was up for it.

Circling the fire, I raised my hand when Cait Toombs looked up from a kiss. She was all soft and twined around Bailey. Her wispy hair floated around her face, shimmering from the heat. Instead of waving, she smiled. Her lips moved, and then Bailey looked back at me too.

"Well, look who graced us," Bailey called.

I flipped her off and pressed my way through the crowd to get to her.

"Dad home yet?" she asked when I got closer.

"Uh huh, this morning sometime."

"Is he okay?"

With a shrug, I said, "Fine. You know how he is."

Cait tried to make room for me, which was sweet, but it wasn't gonna happen. Since we used driftwood for benches around the fire, there was always a free one for the taking. Dragging a piece over, I arranged it so I could put my back to the fire and my face to them. And to the sea behind them, to the fog rolling in.

Sitting, I gestured at Bailey and said, "I'm pissed at you for messing with my head."

Bailey read my tone better than Cait did. While Cait stiffened, Bailey kicked my boot. "Good. Which time?"

I lowered my voice. "I went out today by myself."

"Yeah?"

"Yeah." I nodded, my gaze trailing past them, to the shadow of the island in the distance. The flick, the glitter, was gone. "So I'm getting ready to haul some traps, over on the far side of Jackson's Rock. Minding my own business."

Bailey smirked. "Uh huh."

"I go and look up, and *pow*. There's the Grey Man. Watching me."

Dissolving into laughter, Bailey leaned into Cait. Lacing their fingers together, she settled. She managed to kick my boot again first, though. "Oh, kiss it, Dixon. If you're seeing things, that's your problem."

Part of me was relieved. Legends weren't real, and I was

crazy to think I'd seen one. Hearing Bailey say so made me feel better. There was still a part left over, quietly urging me to look toward Jackson's Rock. I thought as long as the fire burned and the music played, I could ignore it.

"I have an uncle who saw the Grey Lady," Cait said.

Bailey looked at her, amused. "Is that crazy Uncle Jon?"

"No, crazy Uncle Jon swears that time-traveling Navy ship capsized his dory."

Caught up in the absurdity, in the absolute normalcy, I laughed. "What the what?"

Cait shrugged. "I can't remember, it's a city and a worky word. The Manhattan Project? The Philadelphia Experiment? They were inventing invisibility and disappeared in time."

"I'm pretty sure one of those is a movie." Amused, I held up my hands and swore, "I'm not judging."

Cait stuck out her lower lip and blew her bangs out of her face. "Anyway, that's Uncle Jon. Great-Uncle Dalton's the one who saw the Grey Lady."

"Wait, the raisin?" Bailey asked. Then, incredulously, she informed me. "He's a thousand years old."

"He's ninety-eight."

"Same thing. He's the mummy at Thanksgiving."

"That's my family, Bailey," Cait said, but she rolled her eyes and smiled about it. In reply, Bailey crinkled her nose, and I looked away to give them some privacy. As much as they could get making out on a beach in the middle of everybody we knew, anyway.

Before they forgot I was there, I cleared my throat. "So was there more to this story?"

Cait smoothed her knit cap. "Not really. I mean, there is, but he mumbles—"

"And smells like rum," Bailey added.

"Who doesn't?" I asked, and hauled myself up. Dangling the six-pack near them, I waited until they waved me off to look into the crowd. "You guys seen Seth?"

"I don't think he's here," Bailey said.

Then she frowned, and so did I. Seth loved a party, being in the middle of it. Choosing the music and getting people new drinks. Surrounding himself with people kept his light going. After a nor'easter, Seth was the first person out of the house, visiting everybody he knew. Not me; I was the last one to open the door. I liked the quiet. I liked wide-open space and sea around me.

I stood up, nodding toward the fire. "I'm gonna make the rounds."

Leaving Bailey and Cait, I followed the sound of alt rock, lingering here and there to talk to people. Mostly "what's up, how're you doing?" stuff. Everybody in Broken Tooth was fine, it seemed, and none of them had seen Seth.

A waft of steam hit me, full of good smells. The canvas over the clambake pit was still tight. I wondered if I could get away with breaking into it early.

While I contemplated bake robbery, Nick loped toward me. His black hair gleamed in the firelight, long and cascading into his eyes. He slung an arm around my shoulder and took my beer. "Seth said you weren't coming."

"Guess he was wrong."

Ripe with sweat and cologne, he banded his arms around me. Not because he was hitting on me, but because that was the only way to peel a can off the rings without letting me go. "How's your dad?"

It was normal for Nick to be all up on me. He was like that, a big sheepdog who loved everybody. Especially up close. Most everybody loved him back. But even as I let him give me one of the beers I'd carried in, I felt uneasy. "Fine. Sat on his ass all day. Expect he'll be out tomorrow."

"Huh," Nick said. "Miz Pomroy said the *Jenn-a-Lo* was out this morning. Surprised me and Seth both."

I shrugged. "Musta been seeing things."

"You know her. Probably got started early." Nick held up his can and took a deep drink to demonstrate. Then his expression scrambled. Too fast, too loud, he went on, "I'm getting a student license."

"'Bout time."

Brightly, Nick nodded. One brown eye appeared from beneath his messy fringe. "Maybe if you get your own boat, you can hire me."

My skin prickled, and I lifted Nick's arm. Slipping under it, I backed toward the fire. Other people's conversations were tangled in this one. It unnerved me, seeing my life from slanted angles. "Where's Seth, anyway?"

Making a show of looking around, Nick finally shrugged. "Taking a leak, maybe."

Amber Jewett glided by, then glided back when she realized Nick had beer. "Can I buy one off you?"

Already digging in her pocket, she was oblivious to me. A silver vine climbed her ear, seed pearls hanging from loops and catching the firelight. She was in my jewelry class too.

"They're Willa's," Nick said.

"Just have it," I told her, and kept walking.

Faint embers bobbed beneath the cliff on this shore, the other half of the party. If the cops or the Coast Guard rolled up on us, they'd probably figure out that the stoners by the caves were with the boozehounds by the fire. We always kept separate, though, just in case.

The rocky coast rolled beneath my boots. I shoved my hands into my coat, hunching my shoulders as I walked. Leaving the fire reminded me that it was almost winter. My breath added to the haze, and wind snuck down my collar. My back broke out in gooseflesh, the rest of my skin following.

Everything felt slightly sideways. Like the ground had shifted, but it didn't roll like water. If it did, I would have found my balance easy. Instead, it was increments. A tilt beneath my feet; the wind coming from the wrong direction.

No matter what Bailey said, I felt that island. It was looking at me; it felt alive. And that was crazier than seeing things.

Tugging the red-yarn braid on Ashley Jewett's hat, I melted into the huddle. I knew all these people, and they made room for me out of habit. But since I was the angel of death around these parts, it was up to me to keep the conversation rolling.

I held out my hand for the next pass and asked, "Anybody else starving?"

The night drifted on. Our buzzes faded, and there was nothing left in the bake. Slowly, we knotted back up by the fire. It was too cold to stay at the cliffs, even if you did have somebody to hang on. I didn't; Seth never showed up.

Our parties on Garland Beach usually ended with music. Instead of pulling out his guitar, Nick plugged his laptop into an external battery and let GarageBand do the honors. Songs he'd written with Levi—Nick never stopped smiling, but it was a tell. Without my brother there to sing, it wouldn't have been right to play.

"You're quiet," I said.

"Tired," Nick said. He tossed his paper bowl into the fire and slid to sit on the rocks. That had to be all kinds of cold, I thought. He arched his back, stretching his arms, then slumping. "You drive?"

Picking out a piece of sausage, I shook my head. "Walked."

The fire popped, full of mussel shells and sweetened with burning corncobs. Nick turned, resting his elbow next to my hip. His hair fell back when he looked up at me, a rare glimpse of his entire face. "I can take you home."

"You finished my six-pack," I replied. "I'll walk you."

"You should stop being a bitch to Seth."

At first, I wasn't sure I'd heard him right. My fingers stilled, no longer searching the bottom of my bowl for more scraps. Since everything was uneven, and I was buzzed, I blinked down at him. "What?"

With a sigh, Nick slumped against the driftwood. "He's trying to *help* you, Willa."

"Who asked you?"

"Nobody did," he said. "I'm the only one who's going to tell you. 'Cause I'm not your friend. You're my friend's sister. My best friend's girlfriend. I like you, but they're . . . Get past it."

On my feet, I threw my trash into the fire and turned on him. "It's not done, you dickwad. How am I supposed to get over it?"

Nick leaned back on his elbows. "Over it, that's something else. I said get *past* it. It's not July twenty-third anymore. I don't think you noticed."

Replies surged in my throat, hot like bile. Terry Coyne hadn't even been indicted yet. There was a house payment my father wouldn't let me make. A boat I wasn't supposed to fish from, a whole life that wasn't going to happen.

Whether I needed to get past it or not, he wasn't the one who got to tell me to do it. He wasn't from Broken Tooth. He didn't get to judge me.

"I'm not trying to make you feel bad," he said.

Zipping my jacket, I backed away from him. Maybe my voice broke. My throat was tight, my face hot, but I wasn't going to cry for him. None of the things in my head came out.

Instead, I said, "You can't make me feel anything."

"Sorry I called you a bitch." Knitting his brows, Nick draped his arms over his knees. He looked small, but not young. Not even a little; the dark eyes he kept hidden behind his hair were wells, endless and empty and deep. "It's true, though."

I left him there, staring into the fire, because he was right.

He wasn't *my* friend.

SEVEN

Grey

I watch her move through the village. She's distinct from the rest. Her light has shape now. It outlines the fall of her hair and the sway in her step. The others simply gleam, so many fireflies in the dark.

She's seen me. Recognized me. But she doesn't come.

Why doesn't she come? Is there some trick I've never learned? Some secret that Susannah kept when she trapped me here? Standing on the cliff, I try to be a beacon. It's foolish; wishful thinking. Even if she could make me out at this distance, I'd be a firefly, too.

If I were a siren, I could sing to her.

If this were a fairy tale, I could send a tainted apple.

But this is a curse, and curses come with torment. I'm supposed to suffer, and this is a brand-new agony. I spent so many years holding back the fog because no good man, no man with scruples, would buy his freedom with someone else's blood.

Now I realize, I'm not a man anymore. And she's a trick of the light, no more real than a daydream. In fact, she's worse than a daydream. She's a glimmering ring of promises, just out of reach. I can go round and round, forever reaching for it, forever missing it.

Hope is the thing that torments me.

So it doesn't matter that she's thinking of me. That she's seen. That she knows. There will be no rescue. No salvation. And I will spend two thousand years in this lighthouse, twenty thousand, eternity.

Unless I do that thing. I wonder now, why shouldn't I?

EIGHT

Willa

At night, Broken Tooth could be quiet. It was on this side, most of the houses dark, most of the people sleeping. Streetlights hummed and spilled out sickly orange light. It hung in the fog, strange haloes at every corner.

My house was dark too. Daddy's truck was gone, but Seth's was in the driveway. Trudging toward it, I realized he was still inside. I saw his arms, curved over the top of the steering wheel, and his head, hanging.

All at once, I was exhausted. Rounding the back of the bed, I came up to the driver's side and knocked on the window.

Startled, Seth jerked upright. At first, I thought he'd been sleeping. Then I realized there was nothing soft about his face. Every line was drawn tight, his lips, his eyes. He started to roll the window down, then something changed his mind. Waving me back, he opened the door.

But he didn't get out. He pushed the door open as far as it would go. Then he turned to me, still perched on the bench seat. "I didn't know where you were."

"I had my phone."

Seth nodded. He rubbed his palms on the knees of his jeans, then scrubbed them over his face. I wasn't the only one sideways. I could tell just by looking at him that he wasn't right. That he was wrong—we were too.

Then he turned, coming like he was going to get out of the truck. When he moved, I smelled perfume. Clinging to his coat, light and sugary.

A sharpness slid through my belly. All my insides fell, and I thought they might fall out. I knew that scent. The last time I smelled it, the girl wearing it spat at my feet. Probably would have gone for the face except she knew I would have punched her then.

Holding a hand up, I took a few steps back. My voice wasn't my own. It was brittle, full of sharp edges.

"You spent the night with Denny Ouelette?"

Seth looked *caught*. Not ashamed, just surprised to be found out. Grimacing, he stopped his slide out of the truck. Leaning off the side of the bench seat, he pulled his own hair, then took a deep breath. Instead of sighing or finding some shame, he popped.

"I get tired of doing everything right, Willa. It's not enough for you. I can't make you happy, and fine. That's fine—you shouldn't be. But I can't even make it better. I do *everything* you want me to, everything you need me to. And you couldn't care less."

Cold with disbelief, I stared. "So you cheated on me?"

"We just went driving around."

"I know what that means!"

Seth bristled. "Nothing happened."

I walked away, short, tight steps. My head screamed, anger that roared in my ears and cut my brain off from my mouth. Everything I said rolled out, like it was made on the tip of my tongue.

"Get out of my driveway. Go home. Go pick up Nick, he's drunk at the beach. You can talk about how screwed up I am, and what a bitch I am, and when you drop him off, maybe Denny will let you stay the night and be all sweet to you. I bet nothing bad's ever gonna happen to her. She'll be sweet forever."

"Willa, I'm—"

"I said get out!"

I may as well have slapped Seth, because he couldn't have looked more wounded. But he didn't have a right to be sad and sorry in my direction. He wasn't gonna cry. The only time he misted up was at the end of war movies, when it was clear that everybody was going to make it home or nobody was.

His spine straightened. Seth slid back into the truck and dropped both hands on the wheel. He could see me glaring at him, waiting for him to go. Finally, he reached for the key. "This isn't what I wanted."

"Well, this is what you bought."

Hiding under my hurt was sympathy. Or compassion. Whatever it is you feel when someone you love is in pain. Didn't matter that I was part of it, or that he'd brought it on himself.

Because I could trace it all back: I was being a pain in the ass. And I was a pain in the ass because I'd done a terrible thing. So that explained why I was a bitch, and why Seth needed somebody sweet. None of that excused it. Nobody made him open the passenger-side door for Denny Ouelette. That was all on him.

So I watched Seth drive away. I stood in the middle of the street doing it too. Under my breath, I swore I'd be fine.

A fragile, just-been-shattered layer moved under my skin. It's exhaustion, I told myself. I was tired and cold, and I wasn't going to break down in the middle of Thaxter Street.

I was breaking down in the middle of Thaxter Street. I was the one making those awful, animal sounds. My belly wrenched, and my throat clamped shut. It wasn't a pretty cry, a crystal tear slipping down my cheek. It was crying like vomiting. There was no fighting it; it came up on its own.

Seth and Bailey were my constants. My anchors, twin points that came together to be my north. I didn't know how to *be* without them. When I looked up, all I saw was the nothing coming. The future where Seth drove around with other girls and Bailey went off to college and never came home.

That same future with an empty place at the dinner table, and half as many Christmas presents under the tree. The one where I stood on land and watched the tide go out without me.

Nick was wrong. July twenty-third wasn't over.

And it wasn't ever going to be.

Defeated, I walked inside. I heard a TV upstairs, and I followed the sound. Down the hall to my parents' bedroom, I peeked around the door. My mother sat propped against the headboard.

A crossword puzzle book lay in her lap, her place kept with a ballpoint pen. She didn't look at me, but she knew I was there. She patted the place beside her.

I didn't ask where Daddy was. I didn't want to know, and since she was sitting up late, she probably didn't have an answer.

Sliding in beside her, I fit my head in the crook of her shoulder. Somebody else's cigarette smoke clung to her skin, half met by the scent of her soap.

"How was the party?"

"It sucked."

She hummed a reply. Trailing her hand over my hair, she started untangling it. It was an idle touch. One that moved because her body knew how to do it. Maybe we were all stuck.

Those thoughts didn't get far. They crashed into the numb that spread through me. It started at the top of my head and drifted 'til I knew I had toes but couldn't feel them.

Even my voice sounded detached. Mumbling against Mom's shoulder, I said, "I thought you hated this show."

"I do."

It was on for the sound. Or the company. It was on because the house was too quiet. It was always too quiet now.

Squeezing my eyes closed, I burrowed closer to her. I wanted to be ten again. When I could lay my head in her lap and every bad thing slipped away. She combed her fingers through my hair then, too. She used to cure a bad day with idle touches while she read a magazine or watched shows she *did* like. I wanted it to work again.

"Seth could have come in," she said.

I froze. Did she know he'd been sitting in the driveway? An ugly, tangled knot filled my throat. It choked me, and I wished for ten years old again. *Tikki-tikki-tembo, Seth Ar-sham-bow:* that was the worst of my problems then.

It was a relief when she added, "I know it's a small town, but I feel better knowing he's driving you back and forth from these parties."

Shock and tears and all kinds of God-awful feelings threatened to spill out of me. It was on my tongue to tell her we broke up, but I bit down instead.

She'd want to know why. I'd have to dissect it. Sugar-sweet Denny Ouelette being mixed up in it would piss her off. But she wouldn't understand just how deep that cut went. Maybe she'd think it was my fault. Nick did. Daddy did.

Strangling myself on all that, I shrugged. Made myself sound normal. "He had to get home."

Swirling her fingers, she started at the crown of my head again. "All right."

"He said hey."

"Next time you see him, tell him I say hey back."

With a nod, I agreed to carry that message. For a second, my life was normal again. Cuddled up with my mom, the TV playing on. Her fingers in my hair; a distracted message to carry like always. Normal. I had to lie to get there, to myself and my mother, and the whole world.

But it was better than falling apart, piece by piece.

EIGHT

Grey

I melt into mist so it will heed my call. I gather it, from the sky, from the sea. I wind it tight and pull it close.

This is my purpose, after all. I am the lord of nothing but the mist. It's mine to bend as I will—to bring salvation or destruction. All these years, I've held it at a distance. Felt its liquid ache instead of my own blood.

Now I need it. It spills across the water, then rises. It undulates, a living thing. Shadows swirl within it, it makes new shadows. Strange lights reflect in it, exploded to a silvery glow. One by one, the streetlights in town blink out.

The houses huddle before they're swallowed. The cliffs fade—though they're greater than mist and refuse to disappear completely. There's always something greater, something larger—I wonder if there's some earthcaller out there, wondering what's happened to herself. If she's cursed to raise the dust—but somehow, I can't picture it.

Though my wishes never revealed every detail of the curse, it grants me folklore. Myths. I have books upon books upon books. There's a Grey Man on Pawleys Island in South Carolina, but he's only a harbinger. He warns of hurricanes, nothing more. The Irish have far liath, but they abound and care nothing for souls. They seek no release.

I'm alone. Again, more than I was before. I'm taunted; that makes me lonely. I run mad.

So I retreat to the only power I have. I call it all, I bid it come. I beg it stretch the whole length of my light. The air is nearly solid now, a shroud that falls over my island and her village at the same time.

She's blotted out now, and I can rest.

NINE

Willa

I didn't have to ditch school again. It was canceled because of
the fog.

Thick and cold, it clung to the streets. Sunrise didn't cut it;
neither did headlights. Every thirty seconds, the foghorn blared
in the distance. It echoed through the haze, alien and removed.
I lingered by the front door, listening to the radio going in the
kitchen.

"... confluence creating a dew point higher than usual," a
mechanical voice droned.

The Weather Service had a bot, and they could program it
to say anything. It was the voice of the fleet—Mom used to call
it Dad's Girlfriend. *Dad's Girlfriend is calling for rough seas today.
Dad's Girlfriend says we're waiting for a nor'easter, better buy milk
and bread.*

Calm and certain, Dad's Girlfriend told me that I had a couple of hours before the fog lifted yet. That I should exercise extreme caution. That if I had no official business, I should stay home. That's when I closed the door and headed into the haze.

I faltered on the step and hesitated. I really couldn't see anything. People talked about fog so thick you couldn't see your hand in front of your face. It was true; I touched my nose, then reached for the stair rail. My hand disappeared.

Nothing had shadows or depth, and I tripped again on a front walk I'd been running down my whole life. Instead of going back, I closed my eyes. There wasn't much to Broken Tooth. I pictured it in my head—the steps in front of me, the broken piece of sidewalk two steps from the mailbox.

With a deep breath, I took a surer step. Then another, and then I opened my eyes and kept going. My phone trilled in my pocket, and I pulled it out. Another text from Bailey, wanting to know what was going on. I had a couple more, one in all caps. DID YOU DUMP SETH!?

I wasn't answering. Not that one, not any of them. There was an ad on Craigslist for a used thirty-five-foot Brewer in Milbridge, and that's all that was on my mind. It was a junk heap of a boat from the pictures, the hull weathered and grey.

Since it was on a trailer instead of in the water, I wondered what was wrong with it. The listing admitted a blown head gasket; there was probably plenty more. It already had a name in chipped orange paint: *Nevermind*. Not my style, but it didn't matter. It was cheap.

The mortgage wasn't my problem anymore, so I had money to spend. I just had to hitch a ride up that way to get a look at it. And that meant I needed to walk out to the highway, through the fog. Past it. The ground was solid, and it wasn't that far. A couple of blocks to the main drag, and that would take me straight to Route 1.

But my feet weren't as sure as I thought they were. I tottered on the edge of the curb before I realized I'd veered off the sidewalk. Just then, I heard the clear call of a harbor bell. Frowning, I stopped and turned. Water whispered in the mist, lapping at the shore, at the sides of our moored boats.

I'd turned the wrong way completely. Instead of walking landward, I'd found the sea. Stretching my hands out, I felt for the familiar wood rail at the wharf. I slid my feet instead of raising them.

Tension wound around me, tight like rope. I couldn't have gone far, but I was lost all the same. It was hard to take a breath, and the cool burned off my skin in a panicked second.

It was just fog. All I had to do was sit down and wait. Maybe minutes. Maybe an hour or two. But it would lift. The fog always did—no matter how solid it seemed, it was just vapor. A ghost on the water, a cloud too low. It would fade.

I knew that. But my heart still pounded. The world had no shape; I had no idea where I was. There could have been something else in the white. Someone else. Some danger, some evil standing right behind me, waiting. Pulling my sleeves over my hands, I held my breath. I listened.

Another harbor bell sounded, its call twisted. It echoed above me instead of spreading across the water. When I realized I couldn't trust my ears, I sat down hard. I'd known better, and I was just like the sailors that went fog blind. Lost their instruments, couldn't trust their eyes, so they sailed by the way they *felt*.

Sometimes they got lucky, saw a gull or a lighthouse beacon and followed it to land. But there were plenty that turned into open seas and never came home.

An electric wave passed above me. Leaning my head back, I stared into nothing, indistinguishable from the white all around me. Then it passed again, a beam illuminating the sky. The light bounced, glimmering in strange patterns. It didn't cut through the fog; it shaped it.

Standing, I waited for the beam to pass again. When it did, I turned that way and settled. That way lay Jackson's Rock. The ocean was in front of me. The village behind me. It wouldn't take me home, but I felt less alone. There was someone in the lighthouse, reaching to me through the bright.

I swear, I heard the light passing. And this time, it did cut the mist. The fog peeled apart, a narrow strip leading straight to the shore. Water stretched like asphalt into the distance. Hazy tendrils swirled across it, parted by a prow.

A dory had slipped its tether. It drifted against the rocks, bumping quietly as the waves tried to carry it in.

Behind me and beside me, the fog was still thick. It parted just to the water, just to the boat. If it was mine, I would have wanted somebody to catch it, so I started down the incline. I could sit on rocks as easy as I could the sidewalk, holding rope instead of my own knees. When the air cleared, I could sail it back to the wharf and leave it tied there.

I grabbed the bow, my boots splashing in the surf. I'd never seen a dory so pristine. It was white on the outside, unchipped and smooth. The inside was honey gold, wood polished to a gleam. There was a brass and brown compass set into the floor, and no rope anywhere.

The dory was heavy, too, pulling like it wanted to glide onto the water again.

Struggling against it, I backed toward shore. In turn, it pulled toward Jackson's Rock, harder than the tide would take it. Cold water splashed up my jeans. It chilled my hands, and I let go.

There was gonna be an ID number painted on the stern, or a name—probably both. Since I wasn't about to drown myself in the fog, I'd just spread the word.

But the dory didn't wash away. It spun lazily in the water, deliberate, like it was orienting itself. I'd never seen anything like it. It was unnatural, just like the perfect alley that split the mist.

Before I could reason it out, the dory finished its turn. I didn't have to squint to make out the name on the stern. It was a tattoo, icy ink that pricked my skin.

Willa

Humming now, the lighthouse swung its beacon around again. The light sizzled on my skin, crackled in my ears. And the boat waited. It sat on the water like it was anchored, waves lapping around it.

My breath fell heavy as I peered into the distance. He was there again, the figure on Jackson's Rock. It was too far away to make out a face, but I swore I saw one anyway. Dark eyes turned toward mine. Thin lips pressed together tight.

I had finally lost it. That was the only explanation. I'd gone away in my head to escape the real world. To forget the things I'd done. That's why I caught the stern of the boat and stepped into it. It's why I didn't bail when it started to move, steered toward Jackson's Rock unerringly.

Since it wasn't real, I wasn't afraid.

I landed on the far side of the Rock. My head ached, a distant pain that was easy to ignore. My bones knew I didn't belong there, but the boat disagreed. It ground against the shore and stopped. It was strange how alive it felt, like it was vibrating. Urging me to get out.

As soon as I put both feet on land, the dory melted into the fog. I turned in time to see the path from island to shore fill. Hazy curtains closed behind me. If there was a mainland, a sea between this land and that, I couldn't tell. The mist swirled on itself. It parted only for the island, opening up with the slope of the shore.

Pale light filtered through the trees. It wasn't warmer or colder there, but I shivered anyway. Earth and water and the astringent sweetness of fir filled my nose. The light swung overhead again, heavy and real.

Shoving my hands into my hoodie pocket, I hiked toward an opening among the pines. The lighthouse was on the other side. It didn't seem like a big island from the water. On foot, it stretched on forever.

As the pines grew thick, I realized the forest was too quiet.

No flash of animals fleeing from me. No birds chattering from their nests. Branches shivered as I passed; they whispered behind me. It was perfect, the path strangely clear. If trees fell in this forest, they didn't fall this way. Granite surfaced through the carpet of needles and underbrush, the island's bones exposed.

I felt like I was walking through a diorama. Third grade, we all had to pick an incident from Maine history and build the scene in a shoebox. In Levi's box, a Lego Leif Ericson stood on the Maine shore under a Viking flag.

In mine, snow fell on the Plymouth Company settlement in Popham, little matchstick settlers starving under the pines. My brother got an A; I got a note sent home and two visits with the school counselor.

But that was Maine to me. Beautiful to look at, and dangerous if you didn't know it. Jackson's Rock felt dangerous. I only knew its contours from the outside. From beneath the cliffs. Light shone from it, not on it.

The Grey Man is here, my thoughts sang.

And I didn't argue. How could I? I'd seen him, sure enough. I'd dropped my ass in a bewitched boat and sailed without wind or oars or motor. The hair on my arms prickled, then my back tightened. Nothing competed with my footsteps. They were way too loud.

Walking sideways, I scraped my way down a hill and then

stopped. I was small underneath the lighthouse. Up close, it was sturdy and thick, stretching for the sky. It didn't look delicate anymore.

Gears drove the beacon, and I felt the hum of the light on my skin. It pressed into my ears and made me grit my teeth to keep them from rattling together.

And since none of it was real, I kept walking. At any time, I expected somebody to shake the snow globe, to wake me—to give me the shot that would take me back to the real world. Coming around the lighthouse, I wondered if it was a dream. The kind that dared you to wake up before you fell.

Silver curls of fog crept toward me. Fingers of it, slinking from between the trees. It slipped under my hair, cold against my neck.

The haze sharpened—it gathered. Like milk swirling into coffee, curves formed. Shades and shapes and angles, they *became:* black eyes, silver hair. A thin mouth, a sharp chin. A hand reached out to take mine.

"I thought you would never come," he said.

Neither did I. Maybe in storybooks, there's a right thing to say when you meet someone impossible. Or in dreams, because anything makes sense there. A lighthouse could be your church or your first-grade coat closet. But standing there, I felt his fingertips; they were rough. Real.

I was awake, and it was real. So all I had to fall back on was the memory of my mother teaching me manners. Once upon a time in Broken Tooth, when I was knee-high, meeting people she knew on the street. She taught me to shake hands.

She taught me to say, "Pleased to meet you."

NINE

Grey

Suddenly, I have to make decisions.

Inwardly, I tremble. It's too much emotion for my uncertain skin. I feel like I'm nothing but seams and cracks, waiting to break. On my plate at breakfast, I had no box, because I'd wished for a way to end it.

The magic that drives the curse ignores wishes that undermine it. In the beginning, I tried bargaining with it. Every day for a year, I wished for someone to come to the island, all for nothing. I'd written messages and put them in bottles, only to see the bottles melt to fog when they touched the water. I wished for freedom. Death. Anything.

Funny how literal magic can be—last night, I wished to end it. Nothing arrived on my plate. Instead a mistwalk from the island to the shore had opened and let her come to me. She came to me!

She's on my island, and I finally see her the way Susannah saw me. Escape. She's a door to unlock, and how best to do that?

It startles me that she's not just light anymore. Across the waves, down in her boat, she is shaped light. But as I loop her arm in mine, I see every shade of her. She's autumn in watercolor, hair and lips and eyes.

Cruelly, I will never know her fine details. This is yet another delight delivered by my curse: complete isolation. There will be no familiar faces for me, either at a distance or within grasp. I see Willa as if she stands on the other side of greased glass. She's a shape. Colors. Impressions. Nothing more.

If she's beautiful, I cannot discern it. Perhaps a blessing; if she's ugly, I don't know that, either.

"Come in," I say, and she nods.

She's no delicate thing in a wispy gown. She wears breeches and boots and doesn't trail behind me. I know things have changed in a century. I've seen glimpses through strange windows, but she's here. She's real. She's framed in the doorway to my lighthouse, letting her arm slip from mine.

Looking to me, she smiles curiously. "So who are you, anyway?"

That's a question with too many answers. I'm a wraith that haunts the lighthouse. A son with no parents. A lover with no heart. There must be a right answer, so I wait for her to step inside. Let my home speak for me.

She stops in the foyer and tips her head back. My shelves climb the walls, filled with music boxes. They gleam and quiver. Each has a key that wants turning. Just like her.

Gesturing to my collection, I say, "Choose one."

But she's not biddable. She faces me, a shadow crossing her brow. Though a glow surrounds her, I make out freckles and a silver scar through her eyebrow. Pursing her lips, she says nothing, then says everything. "What's your name?"

I haven't forgotten. A hundred years isn't that long. I can't remember my mother's face or what it was like to walk in the sunlight. There are songs that I know the tunes to but not the words. But a hundred years isn't so long to forget who I once was, no matter who I've become. I close like a clam around my name; that's mine.

"Don't you know?" I ask her. "I'm the Grey Man."

She takes a step closer. "So if I wanted to write you a letter, I'd start it with 'Dear Grey Man'?"

I haven't had a letter in so long. It hurts to want one, so suddenly, so completely. She has no idea what she's doing to me. What she means to me already. So I force myself to smile. "I suppose that's a bit formal. 'Dear Grey' would do."

"Huh."

When she turns back to my collection, I resist the urge to plunge my hands into the autumn glow that must be her hair. My cold and numb flecks away, ice slipping from frosted walls. She's warm, and I want to be warm too.

This is what Susannah felt, when I was flesh and she was fog. No wonder she let me kiss her. No wonder she swore she loved me too. I will say anything right now to get this girl to turn around and touch me again. Should I be a beast or a prince? It's so hard to decide.

Finally, I say, "You have mine now. Tell me yours."

"Is that how it works?"

I nod, because it's easier than choosing a part to play.

She trails a finger on the shelf, then stops in front of a heartwood box. I laid gold threads into the lid, loops upon loops that catch the light at certain angles. I can't remember what it plays, and she doesn't wind the key. It seems like she wants to touch it, but she restrains herself. Concentration marks her; she doesn't look at me, but she does, finally, part her lips.

"You should know. It was on the boat."

Was it? I'm still not sure what has changed, but I'll have plenty of time to puzzle it out. She's here now. She wants an answer; she wants something from me, and I have to give it to her. Reaching past her, I take the box and lift its lid. A few notes linger in the drum. "She Moved Through the Fair," of course. How could I forget?

"I want to hear you say it," I tell her, and offer the box again.

Wary, she doesn't reach for it. Much wiser than Persephone; she knows not to take gifts from the Underworld. But my curse isn't contained in gifts or pomegranate seeds. She gives me what I need anyway, the first turn of the key. Something personal. Her name.

I will make her love me.

TEN

Willa

I didn't believe in the Grey Man, and I did. Something, some-body, stood in front of me. With my own eyes, I saw him come up out of the fog.

He brushed past me, and I tried to get a better look. Up close, his skin was skin, his hair was hair. It cascaded down his back like a wedding veil. Its silky wash finished in haze. Curls of mist trailed on all his edges. His fingers. His collar. His lips, when they moved.

"Forgive me," he said. "Can I get you some tea? It's been so long since I've had a caller."

"I don't really drink tea."

He turned back to me. "Coffee? Cocoa?"

"I don't—"

"Then come sit by the fire with me."

When he waved his hand, I saw a doorway I hadn't seen before. A vibration ran through the music boxes. Ghostly notes murmured, running all the way around the room before stopping. Grey walked away, and the weight melted off me. I didn't want to be alone in this place.

The lighthouse was like the Tardis: bigger on the inside. It didn't make sense to have a foyer filled up with music boxes and then a doorway out of nowhere to another round room, but there it was. Warmth poured from it, and it smelled good. Fresh bread and cinnamon. Vanilla.

Neat stacks of dishes glinted from uneven shelves. Brass pots dangled from a rack overhead. On one wall, an old-fashioned stove, black and potbellied, took up the space.

Grey pulled it open with a hook, then threw a couple of sticks of wood inside. He moved like liquid, flowing through the kitchen. His fingers swirled around a dark brown tin. They pooled around a spoon handle.

He was pearly white—not pale pink, not even goth pale. And as weird as that was, what distracted me was his posture. When he stood, he held his shoulders back and his jaw straight. Nobody I knew stood like that. We were all bent over from hauling gear and pulling bloodworms. But even in magazines and movies, nobody stood like that, not that I'd ever seen.

"Two cups or one?" he asked.

"You're seriously making cocoa?"

From a box along the wall, he lifted a pitcher. Condensation clung to the porcelain. It streamed down the sides when he touched it. Pouring milk into a saucepan, he glanced up at me.

"Am I very serious? I could cheerfully make it, if you like."

It took me a second to realize he wasn't joking. Smoothing my hand across the table, I sank into a chair. "How long have you been out here?"

"One hundred years," he said. He put the pitcher aside and reached for a wooden spoon. "Since 1913."

It was too precise, that answer. If somebody asked me how long I'd lived in Broken Tooth, I'd have said all my life. Or about seventeen years. Or a while. And he was supposed to be a thing. A creature or something. Maybe a revenant. Fanning my fingers on the table, I said, "Can't be. My granddad told me about the Grey Lady, and he heard about her from his dad."

Stirring the milk, Grey raised his eyes to meet mine. They were crazy dark; not brown, no pupils. Almost smudges that went on forever, staring past me, or worse, through me.

"That was my predecessor." He gestured at his clothes: vest, jacket, tie. "As you can see, I'm hardly a lady."

My throat tightened. He had rules. Logic. It peeled the soft, curious numbness from me. It hurt, almost, like a skinned knee. I felt too full, trying to make sense out of something that should have been impossible.

Back when the world was flat, sailors fell in love with mermaids. They threw themselves into the water and drowned trying to get to them. But those mermaids were just manatees, fat and fleshy. They looked like finned women at a distance, if you'd been out to sea too long, if you couldn't remember what a real girl looked like.

Isn't that what they saw? Manatees? Fantasies? I wasn't sure anymore.

Grey slid a mug in front of me. Chocolate dust puffed over the rim when he poured the hot milk in. "Stir it quickly, unless you like lumps."

A little bit of hysterical laughter caught in my throat. This was crazy, sitting down having some hot cocoa with the Grey Man, chatting about his past. Suddenly, my heart raced, running so fast I felt lightheaded. Pushing the chair back, I got to my feet and backed toward the door.

"I musta hit my head."

Grey put the saucepan aside. "Then rest."

My body recoiled. All my muscles went tight. My spine felt like glass, and my stomach rebelled at the idea of lying down here. Staying here. The music boxes hummed as I hurried past them. "Thanks, but I'm thinking I should go home."

Suddenly, Grey was in front of me. But instead of stopping me, he opened the door. Pressing his body against it, he stood there, waiting for me to step outside. When I passed him, I shivered. I felt him; he was solid. But he was cool and soft, too . . . like walking into fog.

"Don't you want something from me?" he asked.

Barely down the steps, I stumbled, then righted myself. His voice was a whisper. It slipped into my ear, twisting through my head. *All good days, no bad weather,* I thought. I pressed my lips together to keep that wish from getting out. To answer him, I shook my head.

He didn't follow. He didn't even reach for me. The dark smudges of his eyes were wells of sadness, an uncontained grief spilling over. That made his smile, faint as it was, frightening. "Go if you must."

The path through the trees opened as I bolted for them. I didn't know what I was running from. The island or myself; a bad dream. A bad trip. But not him, because somehow, my skin and bones both knew he wouldn't follow. As I tripped and stumbled my way through the brush, I clapped a hand over my mouth.

I was afraid I would talk out loud. Ask for magic. Beg for that good season, and I was afraid I wouldn't be able to stop myself. If he was real, he would hear.

The panic in my head howled, screaming rules for superstition at me. Genies took your wishes the worst kind of literal. Faeries were monsters; I needed a piece of iron. I needed to get myself together.

When the tree line opened to the shore, I skidded on the stones. My tennis shoes were slick, and I hit the ground hard. Lungs clamping down, I lay there, hurting, not breathing. The ground was so cold, the stones sharp. When I pushed onto hands and knees, a warm ribbon of blood flowed down my arm. Shivering, I raised my head.

There, in the parted mist, was the boat. Waiting for me. No mistake about it. My name flickered on the stern, kissed by cold October seas. I stood and looked back. The fog had filled in behind me. It was a wall, grey and impenetrable. If he was watching me, I'd never know.

Except I did know. I felt it. I felt him, a nagging sensation, like a stone in my shoe. Squeezing my eyes closed, I stepped into the boat and prayed all the way home.

My phone was burning up. As soon as I set foot on the mainland, it chirped for about a minute straight.

Texts popped up one after the other, and a missed call. **Where are you? Are you there? Hey! Are you ignoring me?** Those were from Bailey, and then two from Seth that both said, **Are you there?** Missed call, missed call, then my mom all in caps: **COME HOME RIGHT NOW.**

The fog had burned off enough that I could. Haze hung like

banners between the houses, but the streets were clear again. My phone said it was almost six, but that didn't seem possible. I wasn't gone that long. I wasn't even gone long enough for a cup of cocoa.

Shadows stretched long and crept around corners, and as I hiked it toward home, lights went on all down the street.

They glowed in the mist, some sherbet orange, others sick green. Had to do with the insides of the bulbs, Mom said, the gas they pumped into them. But to me, it looked like a swaying string of faery lights.

My front porch glowed silver, a white light pure and diffuse. I didn't dig for my key. Nobody in Broken Tooth locked their doors. Pushing the door open slowly, I hoped for an empty living room. Maybe they went to dinner. To the police station. To the movies.

No such luck. My mother shot off the couch, all but dragging me inside. "Oh, look at this. You just stroll in like how-you-do! Where have you been, Willa?"

"Milbridge," I said. The lie came out easy. "There's a boat for sale . . ."

"And you couldn't call us?"

"No signal."

Mom's eyes widened. She stepped back, raking me with a look. Dark circles ringed her eyes, and her mouth was pale and tight. "Is that blood?"

Automatically, I clapped a hand over the cut on my arm. "I fell. It's nothing."

"Where were you really, Willa?"

Ducking my head, I tried to push past her. "I told you, Milbridge."

When Mom grabbed my elbow, her hands were cold and rough. They could be gentle; she was about the best in the world when you were sick. Knew when to pet you and when to leave you alone. Most people don't get that balance down.

Right then, though, she was mad. Hauling me into the kitchen, she let go when her feet hit linoleum. Snatching an envelope from the counter, she turned and shoved it at me. When I opened it, a fan of papers unfurled. They smelled like a stranger's cologne.

"That's your summons," Mom said, reaching for the phone on the wall. "They're going to serve you at school tomorrow, and you'd better be there."

My fingers trembled as I unfolded the papers. I didn't understand the way it was written out. There were TOs and FROMs and REGARDINGs, but the title made it pretty clear. I had a court date so they could take my fishing license. Even though I'd known it was coming, it felt like a blow.

Slumping against the wall, I flipped through the pages. The gist was all there. I was accused of cutting off Terry Coyne's gear, and I had to appear. My date was before his. I had to go to court before he did.

That's how it was, huh? Everything moved real fast for cut-off lobster gear. But if you walked out of shadows and fog and shot somebody, you got to lollygag around town, turned out on bail. For months. Maybe forever. I hated him so much.

"Your father's been out looking for you in this. And now he's not answering *his* phone."

"Sorry," I said.

Mom pulled a hand through her hair, then twisted it tight. It smoothed the lines from her forehead but opened her eyes too wide. The whites ringed the irises. She was a deviled version of my mother, brittle and frightening. Swollen with a held breath, she exhaled in a rush. "This family is falling apart."

I stood there, stuffing the summons into its envelope again. She wasn't wrong, and I didn't know how to fix it. If it even could be fixed. Time wasn't going to go backwards. Levi wasn't going to come home. Everything broke at that seam.

"I'm sorry," I said, and I was.

"You don't want to hear it," Mom said, turning away from me. She watched my reflection in the window, meeting my eyes exactly in the glass. "Your dad doesn't either. But I think you ought to own up to the judge."

I managed a wounded sound, but Mom talked over me.

"The fine's not that much, and three years isn't that long." Bracing her hands on the counter, she stretched between them. "You heard that prosecutor. Bringing up a gear war like she knows something. I can't have her talking crazy in front of a jury. They won't do their job."

Cold realization wormed through me. I folded the summons and pressed it flat against my chest. "Ma . . ."

She turned. "If you don't fight it, if they know you already did the right thing . . ."

"How is it even gonna come up?"

"If this gets to trial, you don't just sit up there and answer the prosecutor. That man's lawyer gets a bite, too. He gets to ask you whatever he wants — no, shut up. You just listen this time, Willa."

Closing my mouth, I steeled myself. Mom pushed herself off the counter and caught my chin between her fingers. We were the same height, so when she studied me, I saw every light and angle in her eyes. She turned surgical, talking to me like a police dispatcher instead of a mother. It wasn't cold, it was precise.

"When you get up there, you need to be broken. They've got to see you doing penance. I don't want one mainlander on that jury thinking, *Well, what Terry Coyne did was a crime, but what she did was a sin.*"

It could happen. It *had* happened on Matinicus, just a couple of years ago. If I went to court and fought the citation, I might keep my license. They knew I worked the *Jenn-a-Lo* with my dad; they knew we couldn't afford to lose the rest of the crew.

But it wasn't until then, with my mother close enough to share my breath, that I realized keeping my license could ruin us in a worse way. It made me sick to think about that man going free. Getting to fish again. It was my fault Levi got shot. So getting justice for him, that was my responsibility. A cold, hard shell formed around me and I nodded.

"It'll be all right, Ma," I said. "I'll take care of it."

She smoothed her hand against my cheek. Her steel peeled away to velvet, and she murmured, hushed, "Maybe you can go to college with Bailey."

It was too much to think about right then. Every single thing I'd planned for myself was over. Trying to figure out what to do instead . . . I may as well have been planning to go live on the moon. Bumping my forehead against Mom's, I squeezed her arms, then slipped away. "I'll worry about that later."

Drifting upstairs, I slid my shoulder along the wall. It hissed and filled my ears up with comforting white noise. It sounded like the wind on Jackson's Rock, and falling into white sheets was like disappearing into the mist. An entire day had passed there in an hour, it seemed. As I slipped into a hard sleep, I couldn't help but wonder: what would a hundred years feel like?

TEN

Grey

Sunlight breaks through my window, and that's what wakes me. Last night, I left the fog to do as it willed, and today, it's decided to dissipate.

The sky is unmarred, a perfect shot of blue. It's so clear that at the horizon it reflects the ocean, just as the sea reflects the sky. The edge of the world is exquisite and endless. Everything gleams—the ashes and oaks aren't cloaked in ordinary shades. Today, they're scarlet and bronze, flickering and dancing on the wind.

Rushing my ritual, I dress, I shave. And today, I pull a grey ribbon from my armoire and pull back my hair. I loathe the length of it, not to mention the way it coils and snakes around my shoulders. I'm an albino Medusa, and scissors alone fail me.

For the whole of 1950, I sheared myself. Each morning, I shaved my scalp smooth. I was horrifying.

The first thing I'll do when I'm free is get a proper haircut. Barbers are fine talkers; I'll listen to anything. Reports of foreign wars or agricultural accountings. Complaints of lumbago, lies about fishing. It won't matter. It will be another voice. Another face. A new place, so much better than this one.

I hurry down the stairs, nearly running. I move so fast, the enchantment lags. My music boxes glimmer, and I laugh—I laugh! Aloud!—when they melt away to reveal the high curtained walls of the dining room. Breakfast will be soft-boiled eggs and toast, sausage and biscuits. Orange juice, grits, and everything I need to know about Willa.

That's what I wanted instead of gears and springs. I asked the air at bedtime: I wish to know her.

My plate is stacked high. Aside from breakfast, there's a bounty. Unwrapped, this once—perhaps even magic has limits. It matters not.

Before me, I have two yearbooks from the Vandenbrook School. I flip through those impatiently, then set them aside. Too much searching. Beneath them lie better resources. Much better—photographs. Color photographs! They're magnificent.

Willa's so small in the first, buck teeth and a crooked collar. She stands next to a boy who resembles her little, but for the shocking shade of his hair.

They cling to the rail of a boat, the darkening sky behind them. In the shadows, I see a hint of my lighthouse, and when I flip the photo over, there's handwriting. It's inelegant, artless, but it tells me so much:

Levi & Willa, 4th of July.

I marvel over my bounty. Yellowed scraps of newspaper announce her birth, her second-place finish in a fishing contest, her survival of her grandparents. Grainy copies of photographs show her on that boat with her brother, with her father, with people gone unnamed. She holds a huge lobster over her head; she's older, wearing a gingham apron, sitting on a front porch.

Spreading the bits and pieces, I find secrets. There's a crumpled scrap of paper with a string of numbers written in one hand, and SETH!!!!! written in another beside it. Doodled boats sail the margins of a mathematics quiz.

There's a list of words in her hand, I'm sure of it. Her letters slope, pencil slashes so pale they're nearly shadow. They make no sense at first. Acionna, Mazu, Galene, Tiamat. But I recognize Amphitrite— Poseidon's consort, a goddess of the depths. Then Thetis, one of the fifty Nereids, and I think the list is solved. Deities, every one, rising from the primordial sea.

I find a note from an instructor:

"Willa needs to participate more. Her interests seem limited to boats, fishing, and the ocean. She has so much potential. We'd like to see her try new things next semester."

There's another, mechanically printed, that ends with "All things considered, we feel the jewelry-craft class will be less emotionally demanding for her during this difficult time."

As I clear my plate, it fills with breakfast. Between bites, I create a timeline. Trailing papers and pictures from one end of the table to the

other, I study this recorded history. This proof of her, this trove of details to teach me the role to play with her.

When I finally step away from the table, I'm full with her. My head
pulses, expanding to make room for Willa, whose last name is Dixon,
whose birthday comes eight months after her parents' anniversary. And
who, according to an essay she wrote for ninth-grade English, wants to
live and die on the water.

I can grant that wish.

ELEVEN

Willa

The only reason I went to school was to get served. I waited until the last minute and walked there alone. I kinda hoped they'd find me before first period. Partly to get it over with, partly because I didn't want people talking about it. Looking at me. Whispering about me. Vandenbrook was tiny and full of people I didn't want to see.

They fell in and out of my orbit, Seth in my English class, Nick with his locker near mine. I kept catching flickers of gold hair, Denny Ouelette floating through the halls a split second ahead of me.

The only person I wasn't avoiding was Bailey, and she caught up with me between classes. She had her hardheaded look on. Usually, she broke it out when something had to get done. I think in another life, she was probably a drill sergeant. I wondered what she thought she needed to do with me.

Pulling out the Milky Way bracelet I made, I offered it to her. "It's done. You can have it." I didn't give her the chance to say anything. If I talked fast and talked first, she wouldn't get to lecture me. I was about tired of getting corrected. I was tired of everything, to be honest. "Or give it to Cait. You know. Whatever."

Bailey frowned, rubbing the beads between her fingers. "I'll keep it. Thanks."

"I'm going to sit out front for lunch. You want to come?"

She fell into step with me, still bothering the bracelet as she walked. It was an absent touch, the same way she rubbed the hems of her sleeves when she was thinking. I threw the door open, walking into the crisp cold. The wind tasted clean, and it swept the extra heat from my skin.

Best of all, I couldn't see Jackson's Rock. I'd almost convinced myself that the boat, that Grey, was a vivid dream and nothing else. Seeing the lighthouse would ruin that; it was too real to ignore.

Sitting on the top step, Bailey dug into her backpack for her lunch. "I texted you about a million times yesterday."

I took my place next to her and stole a stick of her celery. I had my own lunch, but for some reason, Bailey's always tasted better to me. "Yeah, I know, I'm sorry. It was a messed-up day."

"Mine too," she said.

"What's wrong?"

Cracking open a plastic container, Bailey stirred her pasta salad with a fork, then sighed. "You have enough going on."

"So? Talk to me."

She hesitated. And I realized she was fighting with herself about this. That she had something eating at her and she didn't want to say. I felt bad, because she was my best friend. She needed somebody to talk to, too, and I'd blown her off completely. Twisting around, I nudged her. "Bay."

"Cait's up and decided she's going to apply to USC," she said. She stabbed her pasta, then put the container aside hard.

Surprised, I said, "I thought you guys had a plan."

"Yeah, me too." The bitterness in her voice clung to her. Eyes flashing, she picked up her lunch again just to abandon it. "She says it's a better school for what she wants to do. And I'm, like, why didn't you say something before?"

"Why didn't she?"

"She didn't want to hold me back."

Slinging my arm around her, I slid in close. "So you broke up?"

"No, but we're going to." Bailey swiped a knuckle across her cheek, then looked into the distance. She was so far away in her eyes, and she looked painfully small. "I'm not stupid. Three thousand miles apart is too much."

"That's a year and a half away, though."

"It's an expiration date."

Uselessly hopeful, I said, "Maybe she won't get in."

Bailey paid that about as much attention as it deserved: none. Waving her hand, she said, "I can't . . . It's like saying, okay, I'll love you for exactly this long, but then it stops."

I leaned my head against hers. It's not like she wasn't making sense. But I grasped for her anyway. If everything was over for me, then that's just the way it was. For Bailey, I could be the one who punched at the moon and expected to hit it. "You guys are happily ever after. It's gonna work out."

"And then they never saw each other again, the end. Some fairy tale." She wiped away another tear, then stiffened. In an instant, she put herself back together. "There's somebody coming."

She had ears like a bat; she must have heard footsteps on the stone walk, because there wasn't anything to see just yet. Though I tightened with anticipation, I kept my attention on Bailey. Since we didn't know who was coming, I lowered my voice to a whisper. "I'm not trying to talk you out of it, boo. I just hate it for you, you know?"

"You want to hear something stupid?" she whispered back.

"Always."

Posed at attention, she watched the walk. "I wish you *could* talk me out of it. Stop everything at the bonfire, and stay there forever."

That was the last place I wanted to spend my eternity, but I kept that to myself. The wind kicked up; it made the forest shiver around us. A dark figure finally appeared on the walk. A woman in a Statey uniform approached us, her hips heavy under her gun belt. I knew what she was after, so I stood up.

"What the . . . ?" Bailey murmured.

When the deputy saw us, she moved a little faster. She put a hand on her holster too. I wanted to snort because Bailey and I, we looked real dangerous with our backpacks and school books.

"Hey, ladies," she said. "Know where I can find Willa Dixon?"

"That's me."

Without too much discussion, she checked my ID, then gave me a thick envelope. Since I knew what was inside, I shoved it in my back pocket. Like an idiot, I thanked her—like I was thrilled to get served and couldn't wait to go to court. But inside, I felt empty, kind of a relief. The struggle was gone. Maybe it was shock, or maybe I was past caring.

"It's just court stuff," I told Bailey as the deputy disappeared down the path again.

"You okay?"

"Fine." Reaching past her, I picked up her pasta salad and stole a couple of bites. "You wanna go sugar Cait's tank?"

Bailey made a funny sound, amused and resigned. Shaking

her head, she leaned back on her elbows instead of reclaiming her lunch. "I don't know. Ask me after we break up."

With a look over my shoulder, I asked, "You wanna let the air out of Seth's tires, then?"

"No, dummy." She kicked my foot. "Neither do you."

"Yeah I do. Let's see him go driving around with Denny on four flats."

"He'll just put her on the handles of his ten-speed."

The mental picture that conjured actually made me laugh. The sound surprised me; it felt strange the way it echoed in my chest. We settled back. Cool wind washed over us again, and we sighed at the same time. We had an expiration date too, but we weren't gonna discuss it.

Instead, after a long stretch of quiet, I said, "We could steal *her* brakes for your tru—"

"Shut it," Bailey said, and squeezed my hand.

After school, I swung by the house to get my worm-digging gear. I tossed my copy of the summons on the table so Mom would know I got it, then headed right back out.

That junk heap in Milbridge was still for sale. It was gonna need a lot of expensive work. Rebuilding an engine wasn't cheap. Neither was buying a new one outright.

The fog had lifted and the tide receded. Hunched backs lined the horizon, other diggers already at work. The mud closest to the shore was already raked to bits.

I had to hike out a ways to find a fresh patch, the mire doing its damnedest to pull off my boots. The cold cut right through the rubber, sending a chilled ache through my bones.

The lighthouse seemed to hover at the edge of my sight, but I refused to raise my head. It was finally a clear day, and I didn't want to see Grey standing on the cliffs. If he was there without any mist in the air, I couldn't call him a hallucination. I'd have to admit he was real. Somehow, it was easier to believe I was losing my mind.

A white boat drifted in the distance, probably my dad. I couldn't make out the details that far away. I just had a feeling.

Lots of boats were white, but this one idled near where I dropped our pots when I was out. Someone moved on its deck, then ducked inside. The boat sped a little ways, stopping again.

That had to be him, fishing alone. Slowly, he disappeared into the island's shadow.

I rubbed the knot out of my throat, then got to raking. Icy flecks of mud spattered me, stinking with decay and dead fish. It was harder than usual. Like I didn't have my usual strength or stamina. Sure, the mud was cold, but except for the dead of summer, it always was.

My rake cut smooth but uncovered nothing. Sandworms, some mussels, but that was about it. I picked up my gear and moved farther out. Just as I bent to work another row, a man called out. "Hey, Gingham!"

Glancing at my apron, I straightened. The guy yelling at me was thin and gangly, his chin so narrow, his blond goatee hung from it like moss. I didn't recognize him at all. "What?"

"How about you move on? Some of us are working for a living."

"What makes you think I'm not?"

He pointed his rake at me. "You got a lobster license, dontcha?"

"Excuse me?"

"I seen you in the papers," he said. Casually, like *most* people got their picture in the *Bangor Daily*. Holding a worm up to the light, he inspected its pale pink body before looking at me again. "Get real territorial when it comes to *your* money, am I right?"

Stiffening, I muttered, "Whatever."

The tide only stayed out so long. The guy bent over again, back to work raking, but talking, too. "It ain't right. I can't go hop your boat and start pulling traps. So what are you doing down here in my kitchen, huh?"

My mouth was dry, and a sour taste came up in my throat.

I wanted to throw things at him. Yell until my voice blew out, because what did he know? I wasn't going to be lobstering for a long time.

All my confidence that a jury would let me keep my license was for nothing, because I was giving it up. Cutting off my own hands. So if I wanted to dig worms or clams or ghost shrimp, what was it to him, anyway?

"Got nothing to say for yourself?" he asked, pulling another worm as long as his forearm. "Not even a how-you-do?"

"Working, same as you."

He snorted, dropping his bounty in his bucket.

I swung my rake hard. When it cut the mud, it sang. One high note, again and again. Grey turned black, turning heavily, revealing nothing. Moving down, I tried yet another spot. Every so often, that bigmouth would yell something at me.

The other diggers moved away from him, because he was breaking an unspoken agreement. This job, it was supposed to be quiet. Nobody telling you what to do. Heads down, rakes flying, worms adding up—if bait catching had a factory, it was the mud flats, and it wasn't for socializing. Or being a dick.

"How many you got, Gingham?" he called.

Finally fed up, somebody else yelled at him to shut up.

Lapping back in, the tide washed around my ankles. It brought fog with it, the thin, hazy kind that swirled when you stepped through it. I wanted to lay down and let the mud swallow me, the water cover me. The mist would be a pale blanket; it might even be peaceful.

My bucket was mostly empty, and suddenly, I was too tired. I splashed back to shore, heavier with every step.

A hot shower washed the mud away, but not the rest. I opened my bedroom window to let in the cold, then fell into bed. Nobody moved downstairs, my father still on the water and my mother back on night shift.

I listened for the creak from the stairs. If Levi had been coming home, I'd have heard it. One long, drawn-out creak and then my doorknob rattling. I wanted it so badly. I wished it hard, throwing it to the wind like dandelion fluff.

A beam of light swept through my window. The lighthouse had kicked on; the lighthouse of impossible geometry, where Grey lived. Where he was waiting for me. Rolling off my bed, I went to the window and stared at Jackson's Rock.

I couldn't remember seeing it from my house before.

Before I thought too hard about it, I put on my coat and my boots and headed for the shore again. I twisted my wet hair into a messy knot and fixed it with a pencil from my pocket.

The fog wasn't heavy; the boats coming back to the wharf were clear enough. I saw bodies moving on the pier, the cut of gulls through the air.

But an alley still opened in it, and the boat with my name drifted to shore. I stepped inside and didn't look back.

ELEVEN

Grey

I meet her when she lands.

This time, I felt the walk open from shore to shore. This time, I see the boat she thinks I sent for her. It bears her name, just as she claimed. A bit of unexpected magic; the curse working in my favor for once.

Offering her my hand, I say, "You're in time for dinner."

The shade where her eyes should be is brown. Now, there are shades of gold in there, hints of black, but mostly, brown. She's still no more than a smear of colors. When she looks at me, I wonder what she sees.

When I set eyes on Susannah, I was wrecked. Every ethereal thing about her enchanted me. Nonetheless, feminine beauty is hardly the same as masculine appeal. I could be unnerving, to Willa. Perhaps terrifying. I squeeze her hand and tuck it in the crook of my elbow.

"I'm glad you came back."

"I don't even know if you're real," she says.

"In what sense?" I look to her as I lead her through the darkened forest. The leaves have started falling, promising the end of the season. They whisper as they flutter, and their bared trees arch above us, a skeletal canopy.

Willa digs her fingers into my arm. How could she doubt my existence? She's touching me. And then I draw a half-hitched breath, because she's touching me. It's been a hundred years since anyone's touched me.

There's no chance she realizes the import of her hand on my arm. She doesn't consider me, not even with a sideward glance. Her light wavers as she speaks. I wonder if she's rolling her lips. If they're full or chapped . . . if they're in need of a kiss.

"In the sense of, you're a ghost. You're a story people tell. If you can get to the Grey Man, he'll give you the best fishing you've had in your life."

"You want me to help you fish?"

She barks with laughter. "I'm saying that's what you're supposed to do."

It sounds vaguely familiar. But there are constraints to the wonders I can work. I wish for things to appear on my plate at breakfast; I call and dismiss the fog. I collect the souls of those few who die beneath the reach of my lamp. It is a limited palette, I admit. Mostly shadows and shade. Still, I've read her life, every bit that's been recorded.

Covering her hand with mine, I say, "Let us agree to always tell each other the truth."

"I'm sorry," she says, frowning. "What?"

I move in front of her, stopping her just at the edge of the woods. There's no moonlight to play on me here. I am as ghostly or as real as she wishes me to be, I suppose. "I won't lie to you. From my lips, to your ears, I swear—it will always be the truth."

Perhaps it was too ardent a promise. She takes a step back, wary. I must do something to keep her. I must entice her, and she's not so simple as I was. She wants more than a pretty siren on a cliff, promising her love.

"I know you're suffering," I say. More truthfully, I can guess that she is. She has to be; I read all the newspapers with her name in them. Until this summer, she was entirely ordinary. But this year, this summer, is a tapestry, and I alone see the threads in its weave. I understand more about her than she can possibly know. "I'm sorry about your brother."

Her light hardens, the shades ceding to white as she becomes steel. "I don't wanna talk about Levi."

"Is that strictly true?"

The fog fills around us, capturing strange lights in its depth. It glows, draping the forest in its ephemeral shape. Willa turns, staring at the path behind her. It's still clear. If she wishes to take to the boat again, to steer herself home, I won't stop her.

I think it's plain by now. If she's a romantic, it's the secret sort. I won't win her by force or insistence. Instead, I ask again, an intimate murmur made for her alone.

"Is it, Willa?"

"I killed him, you know."

Reaching out, I brush my fingers against her light, where her shoulders should be. My words I select with care—the sentiment she wants to hear, not the truth she may need to. That's what her family and friends are for. It's hardly my fault they're failing.

I slip closer and say, "I know you did."

Like frost, she melts.

TWELVE
Willa

Grey listened.

That's what he had going for him; he listened and didn't argue with me. I followed him to the lighthouse, and we sat in chairs that weren't there last time. The music boxes quivered around us. I was afraid they might start playing on their own.

It felt like confession, telling him everything in my head. Every place where I could have stopped. Changed my mind. Every bad decision that added up to Levi breathing his last on the wharf. Right then, nothing else mattered, not the stuff that happened before or everything that came after.

I said everything out loud. Finally, all of it, even down to wishing Dad hadn't quit smoking. I didn't know how much that bothered me, until I said it out loud. My lips burned, and I looked up at Grey.

"You think I coulda said something useful," I told him. "I froze up. In all the ways that count, Levi was alone. He died alone."

"I suppose he did," Grey said. He sat quietly, watching me. Waiting.

It unnerved me when nothing else came out. He didn't try to comfort me, and I had nothing else to say. Silence spread inside me. I was tired of myself, hashing it all out. Standing, I looked for the staircase—I knew I'd seen one. It was a lighthouse; it had to have one. "So you live here?"

Rising, Grey touched my shoulder, turning me like he knew exactly what I wanted to see. And he did, because when I came all the way around, the staircase was there, spiraling up and away.

My breath sputtered; it was impossible. But it didn't feel like a hallucination anymore. Not a dream or a break from reality. It was another place, for sure. But not an imaginary one.

"Let me give you the tour."

He took the rail and started upstairs. He was something to look at from the front or the back. But from behind I saw the marble smoothness of his neck. It was stone white, his silvery hair restrained with a ribbon just a shade darker. His clothes were crisp, that collar looking starched as anything.

And I had touched him. He had shape, and weight—not

warmth, not really. But he felt real enough. Just cut out of trans-lucent silk.

"This is my library," he said.

It was smaller than the room below, but rich. Lamps with stained-glass shades glowed, casting two circles of light that met in the middle. A leather chair gleamed, but it was the chaise that looked like somebody used it. The upholstery was shiny in places, covered by a crumpled blanket.

Books filled the walls, just like music boxes did in the room below. Some—a lot—were the old-fashioned, leather kind. The ones with thick spines and gold bands. But underneath the railed ladder, a whole section was paperbacks. Cheap and battered, they smelled sharp when I touched one.

Casually, Grey trailed his fingers along the hardcovers. "I have a fondness for dime novels."

A Princess of Mars and *Tarzan of the Apes* and *Motor Girls on the Coast*. Yeah, he did. When Grandpa Washburn passed, I'd carried four or five boxes of books just like these to the donation pile. It was a weird connection to make. I had to stop, pushing *The Liberty Boys of '76* back onto the shelf. "How old are you?"

Opening a fat, black volume, Grey smiled. "If I say seventeen, will you ask me how long?" Ghostly brows dancing, he raised the book he was holding so I could see the cover. White hands clasped a red apple.

I stared at him. "Are you for real?"

Amusement played on his face. It lifted the curve of his brows and the curl of his lips. He approached me, closing his finger in the middle of the book. "One hundred seventeen, more or less. I've been dead for the last hundred, so I can't accurately account for them."

I took *Twilight* from him, turning it over. It was the real thing. It had a signature in the front, looping across the title page. It made no sense at all. Waving it at him, I asked, "You get to the bookstore real regular?"

"No. I can't leave the island."

"Then where'd you get this?"

It wasn't right, something real and new being here. I looked at the shelves again, and yeah, he had his dime novels and the fancy leather classics. But other sections bristled with brand-new books. He had *The Hunger Games* and *Freedom*, right next to a copy of *The Devil in the White City* and *The Immortal Life of Henrietta Lacks*.

Slipping his hands into his pockets, Grey came to stand beside me. His shoulder brushed mine, and he slipped *Middlesex* from the shelf. His fingers drifted through it, pale ghosts on the pages. "I can have anything I want, Willa."

It sounded like a curse the way he said it. Like it was a knife pushed between bone and dragged hard through his fleshy parts. Shivering, I put the book down and considered him. "How?"

"I ask for it."

Grey gestured at the stairs, which were suddenly present again. Tucking the book beneath his arm, he started up and just expected me to follow. So I stood at the bottom and waited for him to turn around.

"Maybe you could answer me without all the cryptic woo-la-la?"

"Before I go to bed at night," he said, then leaned against the rail, interrupting himself. "Forgive me for skipping my bed-chamber. I wouldn't feel right accepting female callers there."

Impatient, I leaned against the rail on my end too. I was fed up. If he was real, he was gonna be real. He was the one who talked all big about being completely honest with each other. Lifting my chin, I said, "Whatever, Grey. You were saying?"

"I think about what I want, and in the morning, it's on my breakfast plate. I often wish for music-box parts. But sometimes I ask for something new to read. Sometimes today's newspaper. Once, I asked for a way to see the world beyond the island. I expected a telescope."

"What did you get?" I asked.

"The Internet." He gestured at a desk that hadn't been there a moment before. A laptop gleamed there, a thousand times nicer than the beat-up desktop my whole family shared.

I found myself walking toward him. "How's that working out for you?"

"Not well," he admitted. Holding his elbow out, he waited for me to take it. Then he glided up the stairs with me, his feet barely making a sound. "When I turn it on, it displays newspapers and nothing more. There's war everywhere. Homicides in Baltimore. Missing children, State Fair disasters, a woman who's grown the state's largest pumpkin . . ."

Flooded with realization, I said, "It only shows you the news. A way to see the world outside the island."

"Precisely."

Grey pushed open a hatch, and wind swept over us. Cold and strong, it tried to keep us from climbing onto the beacon platform. We pushed back, and I caught my breath. I was surrounded by the sea. It was green and endless, stretching in every direction.

There was nothing between me and the ocean but air. Nothing split my vision of it. For a screwed-up second, I wondered what would happen if I dived into it. If I'd hit the water and turn into foam.

"Penny for your thoughts," Grey said. Even when he stood away from me, his voice got close.

"I love this." Then, before he got any ideas, I added, "The water. This is most of the world, you know. From space, it's sea and more sea, with a little bit of land to break it up."

Grey's expression shimmered. "From space?"

I leaned over the rail, pointing to the sky. It had started to turn, purple in the east and crimson in the west. Red sky at night, a sailor's delight. "From the moon. We went there. Lots of times. We have pictures from there."

The air sizzled. Grey leaned with me, turning his silver face to the sky. "Pictures from the moon . . ."

"You like astronomy?" I asked.

He didn't look over. His faint smile twisted, into something painful and staid. "I like any view that's not this one."

A bunch of gears clacked behind me, and the beacon simmered to life. Starting dim, it spun slowly, growing brighter with each pass. It shocked me, how much heat it threw off. My back stung with it.

"It's not so bad," he said softly.

He looked across the water to my village. I followed his gaze, and I don't know what he saw. What moved in him when he looked at it.

But to me, it was beautiful. My heart wrenched, wistful. Weirdly homesick. Because it all looked perfect. Nothing to care about from this high up, nothing bad ever happened in that little town. They sailed home on glassy seas with full pots. Everything they planned happened the way they hoped.

Grey put a hand on my back. Its chill chased away the heat from the light. "Willa?"

"What do you know, anyway?" I asked.

Quiet, Grey ticked his tongue against his teeth. Then, he sat on the rail. He reached for me with his wispy fingers, curling them gently against my chin. He was still only shades of grey, but there was a light in his eyes. A dark spark that reacted in the shadows, leaping up.

Finally, he parted his lips and whispered, "I know you're not alone."

That touch stayed on my skin. It crept into my bones and tightened around me like a fist. As I walked home, I didn't look back. I felt Grey, on that island, watching me. I knew he was there; knew he could see me.

From that lighthouse, he saw me. That lighthouse, where nothing but a fall stood between him and the whole ocean. Where some kind of *spell* brought him everything he wanted. As I slipped into a quiet house, I thought hard at the kitchen. I dared it to give me a turkey dinner, to put Levi in the chair across from mine.

But my kitchen was cold. Dark. Quiet. Thick clouds hung in the windows. It wasn't even bright enough for shadows. Opening the fridge, I stood there in a cold glow. I pulled my phone from my pocket and sent a text to Bailey. It was a whisper into nothing, and she didn't answer.

Helping myself to cold chicken and old potato salad, I made

myself a plate and sat down alone. I rifled through the mail. The mortgage I ignored, and I tossed the light bill aside. Those weren't for me, not anymore. Neither was the coupon for a tune-up or a catalog for mail-order clothes.

At the bottom of the stack, I found an open envelope from an insurance company. There was a letter inside, and it caught my eye because it said SETTLEMENT ENCLOSED. Stapled to a letter, a receipt fluttered when I pulled it free. It was made out to the estate of Levi Matthew Dixon.

My dinner turned to cold weight in my belly. No wonder Daddy didn't want my money. I killed his son and paid a year of house payments all at the same time. Suddenly, I wasn't surprised that he couldn't look at me anymore.

I dumped my plate in the trash. I about escaped the kitchen, but Daddy came in the back door. He brought the ocean with him, the smell of it on his wet clothes. He brought the bitter, ashy scent of cigarette smoke, too. It trailed after him like a cloak.

Pulling off his hat, he stared past me. "Standing around in the dark?"

"On my way to bed."

"Your mother bought you a dress."

The calendar seemed to rustle, reminding me of my court date. More weight piled onto my shoulders. What difference did it make what I wore to give myself up? Couldn't I surrender what was left of my life in jeans and a sweatshirt?

Daddy headed for the back stairs. "If you want to argue about it, you can wait for her."

"I didn't say anything."

With a look back, he sighed. "Stay off the boat. I mean it this time."

Of course he knew. Dropping lobster pots isn't exact. I replaced them as best I could, but there had to be little differences. A degree off here or there, a trap too close to the next one in the string.

I could have argued with him. Lied about it. But he wasn't stupid, and neither was I. He wasn't being hardheaded about the boat to punish me now. After my court date, I couldn't get caught on the *Jenn-a-Lo* when there was gear on deck or in the water. The Coast Guard would seize it all. The boat, the gear, the catch. They'd take Daddy's license, too.

"Your boy stopped by."

"He's not my boy anymore."

Daddy rolled his eyes; he didn't try to hide it. "I'm just giving you the message."

Grabbing a bottle of water, I twisted the top off viciously. He wasn't *just* doing anything. It was real clear he thought I had a knack for screwing everything up. My insides tangled and turned, leaving me queasy.

It was easy to imagine him and Seth sitting on a tailgate together. Shoulders slumped the same way, baseball hats pushed back a little too far. Talking all low, short sentences like they always did, waiting for me to come to my damned senses.

Snatching my phone off the table, I took it to the dooryard so I could get some air and to bother Bailey some more. Another message into the air, and silence came back. I texted my mother, asking where the dress was. She didn't reply either.

I was alone in the dark. Not just alone; lonely. Considering the phone, I punched two numbers, then stopped. I wasn't about to go running after Seth. All my emptiness ached. It was gore under my skin, raw and red.

Pulling my hood up, I hiked back to the wharf. The light swung over me, so solid—I wondered if I could catch it, walk across it to Jackson's Rock.

The ocean wasn't the same from the shore now. Earth, solid earth, rock and stone, pushed me from behind. I could walk into the waves, but I wouldn't be surrounded by them. I'd soar over them.

Out on the Rock, Grey was probably sitting down to supper. Making his wishes for books that weren't out yet, or a nice iPad to go with his half-assed Internet connection. All those music boxes . . . all that peace and quiet, surrounded by the sea. He had everything he wanted.

And I was jealous.

TWELVE

Grey

My kitchen is empty now. The stairs, silent. My sitting room nothing but a museum. I have a bowl of broth for supper, and two slices of bread. They go untouched as I flick through the pages of my book.

Sometimes, I realize that my routine is a lie. I'm not real. My body isn't flesh. I don't need to shave, or to eat, or to sleep. When I cut my hair, I'm only rearranging the mist that shapes me. When I tremble in Willa's presence, I fool myself into believing my emotions are sensations.

I touch her, and in that moment, I trust my hand rests on her shoulder. If I were to cling to her or card my fingers through the light that should be her hair, I would believe it.

She would too.

It's magic's perception. All these things I do, I do because they're vestiges of my humanity. I have habits, because I still consider myself a human being.

But now . . . so close to becoming real again, the artifice is never more evident to me. Trailing my gaze along the walls, I notice the edges of the illusion. Those places where I failed to expect something. Mist hangs in those spaces, obscuring the incomplete picture that is my prison.

This, I realize, is why the only room in the lighthouse is the room I'm in. The stairs come and go because I only need them when I walk to the lantern galley. Because it makes sense for my bedchamber to be above the kitchen.

Willa's presence looms. I feel her in every room now. I hear her voice in the grinding gears of the lamp. I see flickers of copper in my kitchen; her chair isn't tucked beneath the table where it belongs. It sits at an angle, just as she left it.

Closing my eyes, I hold myself painfully still. In the dark, nothing exists around me. Now that I understand this, I blossom with a terrible fear. This lighthouse is empty. These dinners are lies. The beribboned boxes at my plate are fantasy.

Now that I know this, now that I can so keenly feel the difference between flesh and fantasy, what will I see when I open my eyes?

With a breath I don't need, I steel myself. Then I look.

The kitchen remains the kitchen. The black stove radiates warmth; my fish broth has gone cold. With my fingers lifted, my book's pages flicker and flip, losing my place. Willa's chair remains askew. The walls vibrate still from the mechanicals working overhead. An ordinary, awful listing of things that simply are.

There's a difference between thinking and believing. I can no more prove myself unreal than I can prove myself real. Finer philosophers and thinkers than I have tried it; some may have achieved it. Ascendance from their mortal remains, existing as pure thought and naught else.

My logic was ruined when I closed my eyes. To truly accept my nothingness, I would have needed to believe that I had no eyes to close.

"I hope you're embarrassed," I tell myself.

Stirring my broth, I upset the sediment in the bowl. It swirls, white haze like fog.

THIRTEEN

Willa

"I wish you'd quit climbing on my trellis," Bailey's mom called out.

One hand on the second-story window and one foot on the trellis, I leaned over and offered an apology through the window. "Sorry, Ma. I was trying to sneak up on her."

Ma Dyer came to the window, lifting the sash so I could hear her more clearly. "Works out better for everybody when you come through the door. My clematis lives and you get cookie dough."

Hopping down, I pointed toward the back, then headed that way. Bailey and her mother were the only people in Broken Tooth who locked their doors. Bailey because her mom insisted on it. Ma Dyer because she liked choosing the time and place when she'd socialize. By day, she did medical transcription. By night, she liked to paint. If it weren't for my mom and Bailey, Ma Dyer might have been a straight-up hermit.

The deadbolt chunked, and the back door swung open. I got one foot inside and found myself gathered in warm, fleshy arms. Even though I towered over her, Ma Dyer managed to wrap me up completely. The kitchen smelled of onions and garlic. The cookie dough was for eating, not baking.

With a shake, Ma Dyer set me free. Reaching for the bowl of dough, she dangled it from her fingers, toward me. "You don't come around much anymore, kid."

"I've been sticking close to home."

Ma Dyer snorted, moving so I could open the silverware drawer and claim a spoon. "That's not what your mother says."

Shrugging, I skimmed my spoon into the bowl. "I bet."

"It's not my business." Ma Dyer shrugged. "But she's having a hard time right now. Try to help her breathe a little, will you?"

Though she didn't mean anything by it, the advice rankled. Since the funeral, there was always somebody asking about my parents. Wanting to know how they were. If I was being strong for them. Telling me to take care of them.

All along, I tried. The bills got paid; the phone got answered. I donated my boyfriend for sternman when Daddy wouldn't let me go myself.

If people didn't ask how I was, that was fine. It was my fault, a disaster I built with my own two hands. People were good enough to keep that to themselves. Still, it seemed backwards that everybody expected me to take care of everything.

I did it because Dixons are proud, and they keep their own. I would have done it anyway. It was everybody whispering it in my ear that left me full of sour, bitter anger.

Had anybody taken my dad aside and reminded him to care for me? I knew Mom hadn't gotten that advice, because it would have insulted her. She would have ranted the air blue about it and probably made me pancakes.

Losing Levi had been a direct ticket to the hall of mirrors. Everything distorted. Nothing certain. I scraped up a buttery mouthful of dough, then dropped my spoon into the sink.

"Fanks for the cookies," I said.

Then I took the stairs two at a time. Photos quivered on the wall, all the way to the landing. Bailey grew up step by step—her hair crazy white blond when she was a baby. With each school picture and summery snapshot, it grew darker. Her eyes grew more thoughtful.

The bathroom door opened, and Bailey padded into the hall. Swathed in orange terry cloth, she looked like a steamed tangerine. Smiling curiously, she tightened her towel. "What's up?"

"Chicken butt," I replied. I hooked a thumb over my shoulder. "Ma caught me on the trellis. She punished me with cookie dough."

With a laugh, Bailey started down the hall to her room. "That'll learn you."

"Won't it, though?"

I ducked into her room and helped myself to the bed. With my gaze, I traced the patterns we'd made with the glow-in-the-dark stars on her ceiling. We grew up with real astronomy: a constant, nagging awareness of the moon, the stars, the tides. So in sixth grade, we made up our own constellations.

While Bailey dressed, I drew outlines in the air with my finger. The witch ball. Captain Jack's rum. The bloodworm. My throat tightened, though I wasn't sure why. We had a year yet. Our stars were immovable.

"So how's things?" I asked.

Bailey pulled a sweatshirt over her head. "With Cait? Still weird. With SAT prep? Still terrifying. Oh, and my best friend. She went and got a little barmy, so I'm worrying about her, too."

"Screw her," I said with a snort. Rolling onto my side, I stuffed Bailey's pillow under my head. "I saw the Grey Man. Up close."

Another snort and Bailey hauled her hair from her collar. "What have you been smoking?"

"I'm being dead level with you, Bay."

"Okay. I don't want to upset the delicate nature of your fish senses or whatever, but here I go. Don't freak." Twisting her hair into a loose knot, Bailey fixed it with a pencil and then flopped at her desk. One of her toy tops wobbled, threatening to hit the floor. Scooping it into her hand, she set it on the floor and spun it. "There's no such thing as the Grey Man, baby."

"What if I told you I really, really have seen him?"

Bailey stepped on the top to still it. Picking it up with her toes, she tossed it out of the way and came to sit beside me. Her hands were still hot from her shower, radiating heat right through my jacket. "Then I'd be really, really worried about you."

"He made me cocoa."

"Why are you messing with me?"

Things were a lot simpler back in our fake-constellation days. We'd believe anything together, back then. The time that had passed had cured us of fantasy, though. Even if I spilled out the whole truth, she wouldn't be convinced. Not unless I carted her to the lighthouse and made her sit down for a cup of tea with Grey. That would happen half past never, by my clock.

I sighed. "I don't know. I'm just mean, I guess."

Bailey used me for a chair. Leaning against me, she planted her bony elbows into my back. Echoing my sigh, she rolled her head to look at me. "You seen Seth?"

"I've been trying not to."

Soft laughter bubbled from Bailey. Digging one elbow in, she leaned over to whisper. "He's pretty miserable."

Closing my eyes, I sank into the bed. Breathing Bailey's perfume, still tasting the buttery-salty-sweet of the cookie dough in my mouth. This room was familiar as my own; maybe more than mine. This is where I spilled my secrets, and I was safe enough to let my heart lurch here. The breaking up was ugly; the being together had been good.

There was more of the latter than the former, so I said, "I don't want him to be."

"Uh, Denny?"

"I'm not *happy*," I clarified. "I just wish things were different."

Agreeably, Bailey nodded. She looked to a faraway place, probably one where senior year and two different colleges weren't looming. She plucked at the seam on my jacket, fingers working without thought. "I liked it better when we had everything planned out."

Didn't we all? Sometimes, it seemed like it should be possible to give up now. To reboot back to fourth grade, when we were old enough to have our own minds but young enough that nothing mattered. It seemed like it should be possible, but it wasn't.

Everything ended: fishing season, summer break, fourth grade . . . There was no comfort in that. So I reached back to pat her awkwardly. Then I picked the one thing that I knew would make her recoil.

"At least nobody cuts the crusts off your tuna fish anymore."

Spasming, Bailey elbowed me in the gut in her hurry to flail off the bed. "Gah, I hate that! I hate it! If you cut the crusts off, it's a goo sandwich! It's just goo, Willa! Augh!"

Yeah, it was inconsequential, but it was nice to know that some things *did* stay the same.

All around me, the world was a secret.

Every door in Broken Tooth led to a story I was never gonna know. Walking home in the dark, I glanced at houses, familiar addresses. There had been enough block parties and co-op parties and Christmas parties that I knew what plenty of those foyers looked like.

But the lives behind them: mysteries. I felt like a mystery too. As much as Bailey and Seth knew me, they didn't know me. Likewise me for them. It was the kind of talk I usually walked away from at the bonfires. You got the Jewett twins high and they were regular philosophers.

"What if we're somebody else's dream?" Amber asked once.

Ashley's eyes went wide, and she held out her hands. Like they might suddenly disappear on her or something. Staring at them, she murmured, "What if they wake up?"

Then Nick dropped a SweeTart down Ashley's top. That was real enough that they stopped worrying about being the spark of an idea in a space alien's brain. It seemed to me like Levi smoothed that over. I didn't remember how. He was subtle.

My brother was subtle. And sweet. And starting to go hazy in my memory.

I hadn't been to his grave since the funeral because he wasn't there. I'd been in his room a hundred times. Mom had sent me up there to get his leftover laundry, so she could wash it and donate it.

It never got washed. It was still sitting in a basket in our basement.

Levi's books, I thumbed through, then gave to Seth and Nick. The manga, I gave to the school library because he always complained they wouldn't buy any of the good stuff. His CDs, I parceled out; some I kept. Posters, I packed, along with his ribbons from school science fairs. The trophy he got for a Washington County talent show. The stack of report cards he kept in his desk, because he was actually proud of his grades.

Those went to the attic. I made his bed. I left the curtains half open, all his drawers completely closed. And I stacked his sheet music on his desk.

Levi wasn't coming back. Every time I went in there, I went in knowing that. He didn't need his *Death Note* figures anymore. He wasn't gonna screw up the alphabetical order on his shelves ever again. He didn't care if I made his bed wrong; it made no difference if I arranged his shoes with the right one on the left.

He wasn't at the graveyard, and he wasn't in that room any-more.

Still, sometimes, it felt like he should have been *somewhere.* Alone, outside, at night. That's when I missed him. That's when I felt absence, the presence of nothing. The first couple weeks after he died, I dreamed him. We were always outside. Walking to the wharf. Climbing down in the caves. Watching the harbor seals on the shore.

When I dreamed him ordinary like that, it hurt when I woke up. It was an ugly trick of the brain. Dreams resurrected Levi; waking put him back in the grave.

He'd always been one door over from me, even when he was brand new. There was a picture of me, all of two years old, on an ugly couch that moved to our garage a couple years back.

Somebody had put Levi in my arms—I was a little kid, and he was a big baby. He filled my whole lap. My hand rested on his downy head, and he dozed away, unafraid. I was nothing but a pink triangle of a nose and a fall of hair.

I didn't know him then. And I didn't know him the last time I held him either. Like all the doors on Thaxter Street, his was closed. I knew the foyer, but the rest was a mystery. It always would be.

Instead of going home, I walked down to the water. Fog drifted in, and the lighthouse beam cut through the night. Sitting on the rocks, I shivered in the dark. It wasn't comfortable, and I was gonna have to bolt sooner rather than later. But I wanted a minute. Some quiet.

If I'd told Levi about Grey, he would have believed me. Probably would have written a song about it. Maybe even waited for me after school to ask more questions that would have turned into a comic book. He probably would have named the character in the book Emma, though. He'd had the hots for Emma Luchies since second grade.

Covering my face with my hands, I breathed heat onto my own skin. Levi was gone, but parts of him remained. Shadows, glimmers—unmade memories built on expectations. For just a moment, I wasn't alone. And then, just as quickly, I was.

Waiting for the light to pass overhead again, I wondered if I could sleep in a town without a beacon at night. Nick said it took him forever to get used to Broken Tooth because he didn't have train tracks behind his house.

It was funny, the things you could live with and the things you learned to live without.

THIRTEEN

Grey

The fog comes and goes on its own now. I feel its currents. I could direct its tide. I won't. I'm not. Instead, I stand in the lantern gallery and watch the shore. All those flickering lights, just out of my reach. All those flickering lives, going on and on without me.

One hundred years.

I asked for evidence of myself once. I wanted proof that I had been someone before Susannah's kiss. That my life was no imaginary thing. And this after I had loathed it so much in the living. After hating my father and his dreams for me. After hoping to flee my mother at the very first opportunity. I wished for evidence of it; I no longer believed I'd been real.

The curse provided. Inside the gold-wrapped gift at my breakfast that morning were two slips of newsprint.

My father's obituary was a plain affair. He passed fifteen years after I surrendered my soul to the mist. He died in his sleep, the memoriam said; he was survived only by his beloved wife.

A grainy photograph immortalized my mother in her obituary. So claimed the caption. The woman depicted there was decades older than I remembered her. She wore black; she looked past the camera.

When I saw it, I felt only numb. I studied the angles of her face. Surely I should remember the sound of her voice. At least one thing she'd said to me. Perhaps the texture of her hands—had they been cool and soft?

The color of her eyes remained clear in my memory, but time had shaved away the rest of her details. After the description of her good works, the obituary said she was survived by a son, missing since 1913.

Until the end, she had hope. Until the last of her, she refused to believe in the last of me.

All the while, I sat on this hellish island. A century past, and I am no better, no greater, no more finished, than I was then. Here I sit, staring at an unfinished music box, suffering an existential crisis.

I'm a frigid, prisoned Hamlet—I have no choice but to be. But I am haunted by the awareness that I cannot be. There's but one in the world that could acknowledge me. The same one that would make me real again.

Longing breaks through my ice; it's painful and bloody. I press my hands to it. Though I know it will mean nothing at my plate in the morning, I wish for the impossible. I wish for Willa. I wish for her to come.

Another voice in this tomb is sometimes enough.

FOURTEEN

Willa

I went to school. Not because I cared, but because I had nowhere else to go.

My mother had the day off. I'd missed the low tide. Somebody had bought the boat in Milbridge, and Daddy left before dawn. Landlocked, it was easier for me to avoid looking to the lighthouse. I could bury myself in make-up work.

The air was molasses, thick and hard for me to walk through. Usually, the halls at Vandenbrook echoed like crazy. If you turned the right way in the English room, you could hear math lessons drifting up from the first story. Since it was a mansion once, it only seemed right. Couldn't have a gothic mystery in a house that was soundtight and echoproof.

But on the day before my court date, the halls sounded

hollow. Voices wound around me, sounding like they'd been shouted down a pipe, miles and miles away.

"Where have you been?" Ashley Jewett asked. She peeled off the wall to walk with me.

With a shrug, I said, "Around."

Eyes darting, Ashley leaned in close. "Have you talked to Seth lately? You know me. You know I don't like to start drama. But . . ."

Though it wasn't a lie in the standard way, it wasn't true, either. Ashley loved drama. She got all the tabloids online, she had *Oh No They Didn't* on permanent scroll. You could tell when it was a bad signal day for cells if Ashley was leaning out a window with her phone.

For twelve seconds in ninth grade, she tried to get a gossip site about Broken Tooth going. Everybody knew it was her, and it wasn't like we didn't catch most news as it happened. She shut it down and rededicated herself to going person-to-person instead. It was tradition, and it worked. Mostly. She seemed to have skipped a link on my personal chain.

"We broke up," I told her.

Visibly deflating, Ashley pursed her lips. She was going to salvage something out of this. "For real, or just on a break?"

As if it was that neat. He still had my DVDs. I still had a bunch of his shirts. We hadn't signed a contract. We hadn't even really said it was over. I just knew it was, and so did he.

Rather than scent the water with blood, I caught Ashley's hand and squeezed it gently. "If you saw him with somebody else, it's all right."

It wasn't. My stomach soured; not that I wanted to go back, but I didn't want to see him *dating* Denny. If he wanted to get his flirt on, he could go to Bangor. Hang out in front of a movie theatre, show off by throwing popcorn in the air to catch in his mouth. He got plenty of attention doing it when I was there. Without me, it would be a silver bullet.

Didn't matter, though. Ashley shook her head. "No! Is he seeing someone else?"

"I don't think so," I said.

"So weird. Because *I* was just wondering why he got into it with your dad at the co-op. Do you know?"

Veering toward a wall, I backed against it, out of the way of traffic. The wall held me up as I pushed a hand through my hair. Twisting it tight, I suffered a strange, cold roll in my belly. It took me a minute to get my words together.

Seth didn't have words with people, let alone my father. Daddy got mouthy when he needed to, but what would he need to go at Seth for? Mismatched emotions competed for my attention, confusion winning out.

"As a matter of fact," I told Ashley, "I do not."

Ashley flumped next to me. It was obvious she was disappointed. "Ohh. I thought you would."

It made sense, didn't it? My ex-boyfriend, my father—I should have known. Just another gap in my life. Another silence where sound would have served me better. Holding up my hands, I tried to set Ashley free. The best way to do that was to put her on another subject entirely.

"Sorry. I heard Nick was getting his student license, though. Maybe that's got something to do with it?"

Brightening, Ashley nodded. "It might. That's a good . . . I bet you're right."

"Glad to be of service."

Before she pushed off the wall, she leaned her head on my shoulder. We knew each other; it was a small town and a small school. But we'd never been close, so it was kinda weird.

Then she made it a little less weird by patting me as she pulled away. "Sorry about you and Seth. I thought you guys were getting married for sure."

I felt a twinge. "It happens. You know."

As soon as she headed down the hall, I started for the far end of the building. First half hour, before school started, Seth used to hang out with me. My best guess was that now he was trying to get as much space between the two of us as he could. I wound through the halls, down to the servant's entrance and the porch out back.

Fully expecting to find him on the other side of the door, I threw it open. But it revealed nothing but empty forest. The leaves were falling in earnest now. Bright gold and copper lights flickered down. When I held my breath, I heard them land. Little whispers that went on, deep into the shadows, and beyond my sight.

Summer was over. Now autumn. Winter loomed, and I couldn't imagine spring. I thought there might be a murder trial then. Bailey'd get early admission somewhere. I wouldn't be running new rope or knitting bait bags or scrubbing barnacles from traps—or if I was, it wasn't because I'd be heading out to fish.

Come spring, unfathomable spring, the rest of my life in Broken Tooth would drift away.

Sitting on the porch, I bowed my head and just listened.

When Daddy banged into the kitchen, right after sunset, I sprang to my feet.

"What's going on with you and Seth?"

With rolled eyes, he brushed past me. He was dirty and wearing new bandages. I could tell all he wanted to do was heat a can of soup and watch some football. The last thing he wanted to do was talk to me.

Still, I followed him. "Must have been some blowout. Ashley Jewett knew all about it."

"Then why're you asking me?"

It was the perfect question. Not to please or defuse me; to drive me rabid instead. There was logic, and then there was Daddy logic. The kind with teeth and sarcasm, and just enough reason to it that it made me feel stupid and furious at the same time.

Cutting in front of him, I leaned against the pantry. "Because I want to hear it from you."

Daddy looked me over. Then, with a sigh, he reached past me and pried the pantry open. He slid me out of the way like I was a sack of potatoes. Mumbling as he ducked in after his can of soup, he said, "Sorry you're gonna go away mad, then."

Briefly, I considered closing the door on his head. Instead, I snatched up my coat and slammed the back door as I headed into first evening. When he talked down to me like that, it made me feel melodramatic. Worse, I hated that. I liked being even. Quiet. I liked things just so.

All this too-big raging gave me the adrenaline shakes. Raising my voice, slamming up stairs, that was about as dramatic as I got. Walking real hard into the night. Maybe if I had a soundtrack, it would have seemed like a montage or something.

No personal soundtrack, though. I heard my feet and my heartbeat and the sea calling me back. My court date waited in the morning. My father waited at home. Not *for* me, just to suck up all the air. So I walked to my real home. To the wharf. To the water.

And this time, I didn't wait for some mystic boat to show up for me.

Nothing was in my control anymore, and I wanted just one thing. The water and me. The ocean. This place between land and heaven that had been my home as long as I could remember —I wanted to master it one more time. I told myself that after court, I'd stay off the *Jenn-a-Lo* for good.

Right then, though, I boarded her proudly.

The cabin stank of cigarettes, and I'm pretty sure of beer, too. The whole thing was sour, like somebody else's sweat. There was a Post-it on the dash, slashed with Daddy's familiar handwriting. *42 pounds.* Not even enough lobster to pay the light bill.

Stroking my fingers beneath the dash, I pulled the extra key from its hidden place and started the engine. One last time, out on the boat that raised and made and ended me.

It purred, mechanics sending a velvet vibration through the hull. I turned a light on long enough to maneuver past the rest of the fleet. Then I cut it and sailed into the dark. The lighthouse warned me away from the shallows and the shoals. Sailing into the night, I put Broken Tooth and Jackson's Rock behind me.

When I cut the engine, a perfect quiet came in. Waves whispered, but no one spoke. No birds cried. I stepped onto the deck and turned my face to the sky. A storm raged on open water, miles away from me. A delicate lace of lightning unfurled. It touched the water and the sky at once. It was electric, and I vibrated with it.

A heavy wave rolled in, raising the *Jenn-a-Lo,* then dropping her. It wasn't much of a lurch, a kiss from the storm in the distance. Dark clouds pressed black against blue, but where I sat on the water, they parted for the moon. It was bright and hung low, wearing a faint halo. That meant rain or snow soon, a near-perfect prediction.

Another wave swelled against the horizon, a brush of moonlight gleaming on its peak. It wasn't a storm wave, nothing like. It didn't chop or crash. It rolled, like a giant had dropped a boulder into the ocean. The swell skimmed toward me. It was slow. It looked lazy. But it burrowed beneath the boat and tossed her.

The hauler bashed the cabin wall. I slid across the deck and nearly went over. All I saw was black water. Felt the spray of it on my skin as the *Jenn-a-Lo* righted herself.

Grabbing the rail, I held on tight through the next wave. My heart beat too fast, making up for breaths that were too shallow. When a boat rolls, everything you see is wrong. The ocean above you. The sky underneath. Water slapping on the deck, looking like it flowed backwards.

I reached for the EPIRB, then jerked my hand away. It was a new one. It would send a distress signal. But if the Coast Guard came, I'd have to leave the *Jenn-a-Lo* on the open water, lost to the tides.

I didn't know why I was panicking. I'd been on plenty of rough seas. Rode out waves so high and white, we called them bed sheets. Survived any number of pop-up squalls. So I clung to the cabin door's frame as the next swell hit.

Everything shifted again.

The stern raised against the sky. An awful cry filled the air, the hauler wrenching against its bolts. Our soda cooler tumbled down the deck, crashing into me. Ice fountained from it, frigid bullets against my skin. Even that was lucky. If there had been a full load of traps on deck, I'd have already been dead.

The boat crashed down. The cooler bounced up and out, flung into the sea. The hauler gouged the cabin wall again, right next to my head. It left a deep welt in the wood. Ice cubes skittered beneath my feet.

Slicked with sweat, I dragged myself into the cabin. Righting myself, I twisted the key. The engine growled, then caught. It didn't make a difference. The next wave hit. Daddy's hula girl, hanging from the radio, went horizontal.

I cracked my head against the windshield. A wave crashed inside my head, this one dark and full of sparks. A hot streak of blood spilled down my temple. I ignored it. Instead, I flipped all the lights on. The radio, too. I had to get my bearings.

The engine was running, but it would be dangerous to steer into the sea blind. There had to be other boats out, farther out. Daddy's Girlfriend would have advice too.

As warning lights flashed, the bilge alarm went off. The radio whispered white noise. In the cacophony, I caught a snatch of an automated warning. *Storm surge in conjunction with unexpectedly high tide causing three- to four-foot waves. Danger to small vessels,* and no freaking kidding.

Alarms blared around me. Taking on water! Check engine! When I keyed the mic, the static went quiet. But no one answered my call. With the lights on, I saw the chaos clearly. Sharp, angry angles of waves ahead of me, peaked like meringue. Then, the slow rise of the *Jenn-a-Lo's* bow, anticipating the strike to come.

It hit, and the boat lunged once more. More water spilled onto the deck. That wasn't enough to sink the boat. The bilge pump was already on, pumping as fast as it could. The *Jenn-a-Lo* was made to stay dry. We hauled traps onto the deck all day long, draining them out the sides.

No, that wasn't the problem.

Another wave struck. It came down like a fist. *That* was the problem.

The ocean, when it was riled, could drown a boat. Not sink it — drown it. Shove it beneath the surface and hold it there. It wasn't sinking if you filled with water all at once. It was drowning, drifting. A graceful submission. Gliding to the bottom to lay with other boats and other sailors, all sacrificed to the great blue.

Trying to find my way up, I gagged on the acid of cigarette ash. Rubbing grit off my face, I lurched when the ocean punched the *Jenn-a-Lo* again. Cords hung everywhere. They dangled like innards, the guts of some black beast cut open. Everything stank: salt and ash, spilled bait, fear sweat. I was flashes of cold and hot at the same time, trying to find my feet.

The mic swung close. I scrambled to catch it and keyed the button. "Mayday, mayday, mayday. This is the vessel *Jenn-a-Lo*, call sign ZMG0415."

The sea answered, groaning like it was possessed. Like it was alive. I dropped the radio and turned. A wall rolled toward me. Black, streaked with silver, it was its own constellation. Poseidon rampant. Neptune at war.

All at once, I was calm. I wasn't going to have to explain what I was thinking when I took the boat out. I wasn't going to have to plead guilty or let a defense attorney tear me up. I wouldn't ever see Seth driving around with another girl.

A sharp touch of regret twisted in me: I wouldn't see Bailey again. My mother. My father. One more sunset on the Atlantic.

Before that registered, the wall came down. I was swallowed by the sea.

FOURTEEN

Grey

I don't know. Usually I don't know.

I see one of the human lights floundering beneath my beacon, and I thrill. Who it is matters not. It's a mystery I can't solve, and I don't try. I snatch a jar from the cabinet. These vessels whisper and rattle, so alive in my hand. Into the elements, I rush.

Though I stay there most of the time, I'm not bound to the light-house. It's the island that contains me. Thus, I can run to the shore when it's time to add to my collection. When someone breathes his last, his soul rises to the beacon road. I open my jar, and his essence coalesces in it.

The whole spark of a human being is a beautiful thing.

I tremble in anticipation as I take my jar and rush to the water. A storm and stars, lighting and a full moon. It's an extraordinary night!

One more silver, swirling vial of life to line the shelves. One more tick off my immortal clock.

But when I reach the shore, I see autumn colors instead of an indeterminate glow. Copper hair, dusky mouth, I see her. This time I know her name. The shape of her hand. I recognize the essential parts — this isn't another light, this is Willa.

I drop the bottle. Its bulb shatters on the rocks, and I wade into the water. When I go too far, I peel apart. I'm red-hot strips of agony, then nothing in an infernal cold. Then I form again on the shore, whole. Complete. Watching her go under.

This can't happen. One more out of a thousand is not enough: collecting her ruins everything. She's my hope. My escape! She's walking on the far shore this year instead of a millennium hence. She comes to me and touches my things. She's real and alive; I need her to stay.

There are no mannerly waves tonight. They roll and crash, making walls of driftwood, pushing them ever closer to the wood that shadows my rock. I can't get closer. My agonizing insubstantiality persists. There are borders to my curse, a gate through which I cannot pass.

So I call the mist. I wind it around the island, wool on a spindle. I hope that it will calm the seas, just enough to bring her to shore. Not just her soul, but the whole of her.

Since the curse has been so very accommodating, I wish. On my breakfast plate, I want proof that she's well, that she more than survived the night. The curse will grant it; a wish like that couldn't be more contrary to its desires.

The waves roar yet, now blanketed in haze—but I see her light. With each surge, it flows toward me. I hold out my hands. To catch her; perhaps to call her. As if I'm some saltwater god and not a monster in a tower.

She can't be lost. I've waited too long. I've been too generous, too careful, too kind. Despite my strange-made flesh, I've been so very human, and it's time. I deserve this. I deserve her, deserve the chance to kiss her. To make her love me enough to die for me. All these things should be mine.

I wade in again, the island sure beneath my feet in spite of the inundation. The next wave crashes through me. There's a trembling, the curse threatening to shear me to pieces again. I'm almost too far out. My contradictory bones ache from the cold, but, oh, lucky hand! I catch a length of what must be her hair.

Winding my wrist in it, I drag her into the air. It's brutish, but it works. Once I've pulled her from the surf, I can better grasp her. I can even be gentle—scooping my arms beneath her, hefting her sodden shape off the ground. Her edges trail like seaweed.

Suddenly, her edges sharpen. She's less a haze of light and shape, and more a girl.

No, she's a mermaid made real, cradled in my arms and breathing! Gloriously, wonderfully breathing! Her face is battered. Bruised and swollen. Her skin cast in faint shades of blue. A vicious shudder rolls through her, and though she's stiff with cold, she curls toward me. Catching my shirt with one hand, she clings to it.

Usually I don't know the names or faces that belong to the souls in my bottles. Like the lights on the shore, they're no more than the flickering of fireflies, single keys to try in the lock of my cage.

But this time, I looked out and knew it was Willa, and I thrill at her exception. She's special; it must be destiny.

My curse's end must be near!

FIFTEEN

Willa

The angle of the light was wrong when I woke up. The sunrise was supposed to come through my window direct. It should have warmed my face, then my neck, then made me too hot to stay in bed anymore.

Instead, a single streak of light played above me. It danced, and reflected off a mirror I didn't own. I jerked up and stared. The room wasn't mine, but it was familiar. A lacy canopy draped the bed—the kind I always asked for when I was little. Glass witch balls in green hung by the window. I'd begged for those at a street fair once.

An oar hung on another wall. It gleamed, perfectly polished. Below that, pictures of the sea. At dawn. At dusk. With a storm on the horizon. In the clear after a squall. And then, the *Jenn-a-*

Lo sailing away, outlined by fireworks. A younger version of me leaned on the rail, elbow to bony elbow with Levi.

The memory of water crashed over me. Frigid cold, it stole my breath. The salt blood of it filled my nose, the room. I was dry drowning, so I threw myself at the window. The glass reflected my ghost self. My lip was split, my eye blacked. I had to touch my forehead to confirm the goose egg there.

Wrenching the curtains open, I shrank at the blinding burn. Then, as the sensitivity faded, I made out shapes. The water, the ground, too far below. My throat seized and my lungs, too. I recognized the view. I stood at the top of the lighthouse. Across the water, my village.

Even from so far away, I saw the destruction in the harbor. Boats piled on top of boats; masts like matchsticks, snapped and scattered. The sun shone too bright. It mocked the washed-out wharf; it mocked me.

A slow throb started in my head. It beat in time to my pulse as I turned from the window. Those swells had swallowed my father's boat. They'd beaten at Broken Tooth, littered the shore. How many of us were ruined?

I pushed the window open and grimaced. Dead fish and algae, seagrasses in the sun—it was a terrible smell. It would take weeks to fade.

Cold, rank air coated too much of my skin. Looking down, I

realized my jeans and sweatshirt were gone. I wore a guy's shirt in the palest green that could still be called green, and panties. *My* panties, thank God. But my insides soured.

Grey's hands had been on me when I was passed out. He'd looked at me, undressed me! My head hurt when I tried to piece the night together. But all that came back was the wave. A tower of glimmering black and then nothing.

Throwing a blanket around my shoulders, I turned expectantly. There should have been stairs, but there weren't. Spinning around again, I waited for the magic to happen. How crazy, screwed up, straight-up damaged was that, expecting *magic*.

Nothing happened, and my pulse raced. I brought my heel down hard. The witch balls quivered on their ribbons. I stomped on the floor. If that didn't reveal the stairs, maybe it would get that freak Grey's attention.

A small part of me wondered if I really wanted it. Maybe throwing myself out of the tower would have been a better escape. Terns swooped against the flawless sky. Shrill cries echoed against the lighthouse. If only I could follow the birds. Fly away home. Fear spilled out of me.

"Grey!" I shouted. My voice broke. "Let me out!"

He didn't answer. I tried again, a few times. Too many times. Until my throat felt raw, and the sounds I made were barely recognizable. He wasn't answering. I'd have to rescue myself. Free myself. There would be blood spilled before I settled down to be his Rapunzel.

Stripping the bed, I laid the linens out. All of them—the sheets and the coverlets, the duvet, and even the dust ruffle. Dropping to my knees, I tied the corner of one to the next. My bowknots were good and strong. I wasn't that far off the ground. It worked in movies, although that didn't mean much.

I secured one end of my rope to the bed. Just as I hefted the rest to the window, the room shifted behind me. Two footsteps sounded on a spiral staircase. China rattled on a tray, and Grey looked seriously confused.

"I brought breakfast," he said, and turned away from me.

"Where are my clothes?"

The question seemed to embarrass him. He didn't blush. There wasn't that much color in him. Sliding the tray onto the bed, he gestured at a stand-up chest. "I'm sure they're dry now."

Edging around him, I opened the door. I yanked my jeans off a hanger. They rasped when I put them on, but they were warm and soft. Cedar sweetened my sweatshirt, surrounding me as I pulled it over my head. I didn't bother to take off the foreign shirt. I could get rid of it at home.

Eyes on the ceiling, Grey started, "You seem perturbed—"

"Don't."

I pulled my shoes over bare feet and snatched my coat. The

hangers swung on the bar, whispering as they rubbed together. Little echoes filled the armoire, ripples in the air. Freeing my hair from my collar, I backed toward stairs that finally existed. Grey left the tray on the bed and turned to follow me.

"I don't understand what I've done wrong. You almost drowned; I pulled you from the water."

His weight made the spiral staircase tremble, and I didn't know where it was going anyway. So far as I saw, rooms came and went in the lighthouse. They only existed when he wanted them to. I was relieved when the next landing was the library.

Desperation in his voice, Grey reached for me. "What have I done to offend you?"

"Nothing," I told him. "No, wait, you said let's be honest."

"Please."

The rough iron rails bit into my palms as I hurried down stairs that never seemed to end. I was almost out of breath. The music-box room should have been ten steps down, but I kept spiraling with no end. "You pulled me out, great, thanks. But you stripped me. You locked me in that room. What's wrong with you?"

"That's the worst possible interpretation. You can't afford me the benefit of the doubt?"

I threw a look over my shoulder. He was serious. He was actually ticked that I didn't appreciate all his creeping when I was unconscious. A shudder raced through me. "What's the *good* spin on locking me in your tower?"

"The truth," Grey said stiffly, "is that I put you in my bed but the lighthouse decided to provide you with your own chamber."

"It's a *building!* It doesn't decide anything!"

"Doesn't it?"

He reached past me and pushed open the door. A door—it wasn't there a second ago. And it didn't open onto the music-box room. Instead, the wind rushed in, bitter with death. The beacon hummed, spinning without light. I was back at the top of the lighthouse.

The dull ache in my head turned sharp. I stepped onto the lantern gallery because I didn't have anywhere else to go. Outside seemed better. I could breathe there. I could back away from him. Iron rattled with my steps. I pressed the heel of my hand to my temple. "Let me out."

Grey drifted past me. He was smart enough to keep his hands to himself. Though his shadowy eyes pinned me, he moved away. Wrapping his hands on the guardrail, he stared at the sea. Didn't even look over once. The wind tried to snatch his voice, but I heard him all the same.

"It stuns me that you think I have any control over this whatsoever."

"You're telling me you don't?"

He looked like a storm coming in. He threw his hands up, flashes of lightning, his voice thunder. "It's cursed. I'm cursed, this place is cursed. Don't you know an illusion when you see one? You woke up in the room *you* desired, dressed the way *you* imagined."

My mouth gaped. "That wasn't *my* imagination."

"I swear to you, it was." He turned to me finally. His hands flew, dangerously constrained against his chest. But they trembled; he was furious. "You're not *flesh* to me, Willa. I see the life in you that I could collect, but nothing more. You're a ghost. You're a lie."

I probably was all those things. And I was afraid. I glanced at the rocky shore below. I didn't have my sheet rope now. No matter how many physics classes I missed, I still understood terminal deceleration. It was too far down. I'd never survive. Nobody could survive.

Grey set his jaw and looked away. "Just *want* to leave and you *can*. Only one of us is bound here."

"Yeah?" I spread out my arms. "I'm still here. And I can think of about a million places I'd rather be."

"You must not want to be there very badly."

If I'd known him, if we'd grown up together, I might have decked him. Instead, I threw out my arms and said, "Wishful thinking on your part."

Instead of answering, Grey's expression darkened, and he

looked back to the sea. He was made of marble. Chill pale, with grey veins that pretended he had a pulse. I bet if I touched him, his hands would be stone. His mouth would be ice.

This frozen creature stepped onto the rail. The wind plucked at his hair. It was mist and nothing more. Wild, foggy tendrils that flowed around his head, then pulled straight.

Grey jumped.

He didn't say a word. He didn't even look back. Over the side, he plummeted without a scream. There was screaming, though: mine. It tore from my throat. I threw myself against the rail, raw with terror.

Clinging to iron so cold, it bit, I leaned over. I was fast. I saw him hit the ground. Exploding into ribbons of haze, he disappeared. No body. No blood. Nothing left of him.

"As you see," he said behind me. "Only one of us is bound here."

My skin crawled. I whipped around, and there was Grey. Whole. Still cold and pale and frightening. But fine as could be, like he'd never jumped at all.

Frigid wind blasted off the water. It pushed me back, and I saw the stairs. I shoved past Grey. My heart was jelly, quivering instead of beating. I almost fell, but I didn't slow down. Taking the stairs two at a time, I ran. Like if I hurried, the lighthouse would have to let me go.

I needed to be outside. I *wanted* to go home.

My footsteps echoed in my head. In my ears. If I did fall, I wondered if I would ever stop. The spiral could have gone on infinitely. My body would tear apart. Smaller and smaller pieces, until nothing but blood and atoms stained the steps.

Tinny, discordant notes jangled around me. Music boxes trembled. A soaring wall of them, delicate brass and silver fixtures shivering, strangely alive. Light glinted on them; it was too bright. I caught glimpses of my face, bent by spiked wheels and shimmering gears. A thousand fun-house mirrors, all playing their own eerie songs. So many sharp edges.

I ran past them and crashed through the door.

Pushing through, I clapped a hand over my mouth. By force alone, I strangled a laugh or a sob. Maybe both. Because when I passed through, I didn't find myself standing on the stone cliff of Jackson's Rock.

I was at home.

I stood on my own front step, staring at the front door my mother liked to paint a new color every spring. I reached for the knob and yelped when it turned on its own.

Daddy stared at me, uncomfortable in a suit. His face looked like putty, the color off and the shape of it just a little wrong. Lips parting, he smoothed a hand over his head. Then, without softness, he demanded, "What happened to you?"

My body wouldn't let me admit any of it. Losing the *Jenn-a-Lo* felt just as imaginary as the Grey Man.

Since I didn't answer, Daddy rolled his eyes at me and went back inside. He called to my mother, "She's back!"

I was. I was home. And I had a court date.

FIFTEEN

Grey

She thinks I'm a monster.

It was evident in her eyes and her accusations. Though I have my own motives, I can't think of a thing I've done to deserve that kind of reception. I've been kind; I've been gentlemanly. I've told her the truth all along—most of it, enough of it.

It makes me wonder what kind of world really runs on the other side of the sea. There have always been passions and madness. Murders and cruelty and all manner of evil in the world. I'm not so naive; I was a fool for Susannah, but not unworldly. Things were no better when I walked free; I could argue they were worse.

But Willa thinks I'm a monster. As if I would take advantage of her in all her helplessness. As if I could be so ungallant—I'm not made that way. I'll tell her what I want from her, very clearly.

I've promised not to lie, because she shouldn't swallow everything with bitterness when she takes this post. A thousand years or a thousand souls, it's an eternity to suffer alone with your regrets.

I wonder if I shouldn't have collected her last night. Given up on the possibility that she would take my place here. I can't seduce her. I can't sweeten her with words. My music boxes frighten her.

I frighten her.

It must have been so much easier for Susannah. She tilted her pretty eyes, and I fell. I imagined I loved her before a single word passed between us. She was nothing more than a figure on a cliff. Her mystery lit my blood; all the rest I'd invented. I'd done all the work. By the time I found my way to her shore, she but had to wait for me to say the words. I volunteered them! Of course I would die for her. Kill and steal and lie for her.

How easily I gave up my heart, my freedom. My flesh.

Willa won't be so easily persuaded. I worry she won't be persuaded at all. Other sins can be rectified; if I had been short with her, or angry, or inconstant. Those could have been cured with apologies. But fear is base. Innate. It's impossible to convince people they aren't afraid.

But—and isn't there always a but—she's the one who thought of me. Who came to me. Who broke through the barriers and landed on my island. She's the one. She has to be the one. I know that she's wounded, but this morning above all proved she will not surrender.

Wonders and magic don't entice her. The eerie beauty I wear on *account of this curse does nothing to delight her. I can't beat against her; she is no shore to be softened by persistence. Tricks will buy me nothing with her. I think, to win her and my freedom, that I have just one course.*

I'll have to understand her.

SIXTEEN

Willa

My mother sat in the front seat, pressing her temple against the window. Her voice was glass, thrown at me. "You feel like telling us what happened to your face?"

"There was a storm," I started. They had to know there was a storm. Daddy would have been at the shore at daybreak. He knew the *Jenn-a-Lo* was gone. He probably knew I was the one who lost her. I was sick in my soul with it. Like if somebody cut me open, I'd be nothing but green bile inside.

"There's a news flash." Ma had a gift for sarcasm when it suited her.

Making a hard left, Daddy grunted. "Leave it be."

"I didn't know there would be swells like that."

Mom turned around. A faintly orange mask of makeup

obscured her real features. Granny's pearls hung from her ears, matched by the rope of them around her neck. She was a Kabuki dancer, painted to play her part. Mother of the defendant. The wine-dark lipstick made her look old and angry. "All night on the water with Seth?"

Recoiling at the sound of his name, I stared at her. "I told you we broke up."

Her teeth were white, too white. Like bone, behind that lipstick. They chopped and snapped, making a sharp breath whistle. "Seth did that?"

"No!" She wasn't listening. She wasn't even trying to listen. She just wanted me to fill in the script she already wrote. "We've *been* broken up. I hit the windscreen, Ma. I was on the boat when it . . ."

"Knock it off, both of ya," Daddy said.

With a huff, my mother turned on him. "I don't think I will, Bill. Look at her! Going to court looking like a prizefighter. And God knows, last time she went running around all night long . . ."

"I sailed to Jackson's Rock," I shouted. I raised my voice to blot hers out. It was about as elegant as clapping my hands over my ears and singing, *la la la, I can't hear you.* The long drive to the courthouse in Machias was bad enough.

A death watch, counting down minutes until everything was

over. I wanted to explode, or to die. Something—some kind of penance for ruining everything. For Levi and for sinking the *Jenn-a-Lo* and for pitting my parents against each other.

Another snort punctuated the air. Daddy flicked his pale eyes to peer at me in the rearview mirror. "I told you to stay off the boat."

"I know." I dug my fingers into the rubbery seat, straining against my seat belt. "And I'm sorry. I'm sorry for everything. I'm sorry . . ."

Then he laughed. It was hollow and terrible. He wheezed when he drew the next breath, and whistled it out with laughter. Sweeping away tears, he drove with one hand, faster on the highway than Mom liked. I was baffled. I guess I could have been offended. Or hurt. Or angry, but he was laughing, and I was too confused to feel anything else.

Not so my mom. She pursed her lips and dropped back against the seat furiously. "I'm glad you're having a good time."

"You and me both." Daddy said. "You shoulda seen the look on Eldrich's face. Like somebody slapped a herring. Can't say I blame him. His *Boondocks* was standing ass over end, leaning against the bait shack. Half the fleet's upside down. Then, then . . ."

He burst out laughing again. The car veered a little, and I wondered if this was what a real nervous breakdown looked like. If all the breaking I'd been doing was just a tantrum. Daddy's face was scarlet, and he kept coughing between his giggles. Mom took the wheel, steering us back into our lane.

"There's the *Jenn-a-Lo!*" Daddy shouted, then hiccupped. "Floating all alone in the harbor. Bell missing but pretty as the day I bought her. I look at Eldrich. He goggles back at me. Then he says, 'Guess it's your year.'"

Daddy was the only one who found it funny. He dissolved into more laughter. And that turned into a coughing fit. It had been a long time since he coughed like that, wet and sticky. Since he quit smoking last time, as a matter of fact. It rumbled and bubbled in his chest, and made me want to cry.

I couldn't even be relieved. It was a miracle that the *Jenn-a-Lo* was floating. Impossible. Magic.

Gripped by an unholy cold, I folded into myself. I wasn't giving Grey credit for saving the boat. He didn't get credit for pulling me out of the water, either. He had to go into a box in my head. Clamped down and locked down, because the things that happened on Jackson's Rock couldn't come into this world. My real world.

The one where we rolled into Machias under a perfect sky. The leaves were almost finished shifting—some still green, but most a vibrant orange against blue. Yellow and white Victorians lined one side, blue and grey Cape Cods the other. The highway turned into Court Street.

The court building was a red brick box, capped with a white

bell tower. Didn't seem right that it wasn't all marble. Sporting columns instead of narrow windows; it should have looked like a place of judgment. Close enough, since it could have been a church, from the look of it.

Now that he had to slow to park, Daddy's laughter died. Mom sat stiffly, shaking her purse like she was panning for gold instead of her lipstick. In the back seat, I kept my split-lipped mouth shut. After midnight in the Great South Channel wasn't so cold, or so almost-quiet, as it was in that car.

I wanted to run. Just fling open the door and tear off. Past the perfect little park across the way. Through the blazing trees, down the asphalt streets. If I kept going, if I ran long enough, I'd find the ocean again. I could throw myself into it. Drown like I was supposed to the night before.

Instead, I folded my coat over my arm and followed my parents inside.

Two seconds before I stepped up in front of the judge, I met Mr. Farnham, a lawyer I didn't know I had. Mom gave me a hug and pushed me in the lawyer's direction. I wavered. Hanging like dew on a line, suspended.

Even though the courtroom was claustrophobic—I could hear two ladies in the back row whispering—I felt so alone. I think Mom knew; she looked like she was sorry, but she slipped her arm through Daddy's and led him to the back of the gallery anyway.

I sat in the front row with Mr. Farnham and stared at the empty jury box. Everything was planned, I was given up to it. But there was telling my head what was going to happen, and then there was convincing my bones.

Sometimes, people walked into the ocean on purpose, weighted themselves down, even. But I guarantee, their flesh fought it in the end. All of a sudden, my life was a case number. The things I'd agreed to do tasted like poison. I longed to spit them out. Raise my voice. Change my mind.

"One-twelve dash CV dash twelve dash WLF," the bailiff read. She looked like she'd had to put a book down just when she'd gotten to a good part.

Mr. Farnham stood and hustled me to my feet too.

Bored and wanting to be elsewhere, it was written on the bailiff's face. It dripped through her voice when she read the complaint against me. Not charges, because it wasn't a *crime* anymore, gear molestation. The complaint. The bailiff's gun belt hung low, jingling a little when she handed the file over to the judge.

Over the folder, the judge raised a brow at me. My black-and-blue face didn't match the navy blue dress my mother had picked out for court.

It didn't match me, either. It felt like a straitjacket, rough and binding. My dress shoes pinched. I wasn't handcuffed, but I kept my arms folded behind my back. Was I supposed to try to look sorry? Penitent? I probably wasn't supposed to grimace when the judge talked at my lawyer.

Mr. Farnham, all shave bumps and ghostly green eyes, nudged me. He smelled expensive, like the country club Bailey waited at last summer. Just one scent, and my head was full of old men and silk ties. Of places Bailey and I had seen together. Of Levi pressing his crooked teeth into an apple to make a jack-o'-lantern smile in red flesh.

Memories stirred and twisted: kissing Seth Archambault in my mama's kitchen, stories about the October storm that Mom and Dad missed because of their wedding. The first time I earned a hundred-dollar bill; learning to plot strings into the GPS.

Dixon names carved into the newel post at school, a hundred years ago. Eighty, sixty, forty, twenty — and mine, fresh and new.

"Willa," the lawyer said. He turned to whisper behind my ear. "The judge asked if you're entering a plea. Now you say, 'Yes, your honor.' Then she'll ask *what* you plead."

I stepped off a ledge. "Guilty," I said.

It was hard to tell if the judge cared that I went out of order. Flipping papers, she barely looked up at me. "Am I to take it to mean that you would like to admit liability?"

Voices exploded behind me. I recognized my father's baritone in them, and turned. His face was red, and he whispered furiously to my mother. A few people around them murmured. I saw their lips moving, but couldn't make out a word.

The judge didn't shush them. She talked over them. "Mr. Farnham, Miss Dixon?"

Rattled, my lawyer looked back to my parents before addressing the judge again. "Yes, ma'am, that is, we are . . ."

"You understand that by admitting liability, you'll forfeit your right to an appeal. That your fishing license will be suspended for three years. That you will be responsible for all fines levied against you."

Daddy dropped an F-bomb, standing up and raising his voice. I don't know what he was going to say. The judge cut him off, regal and unruffled. "You can wait outside, sir."

"Your honor," Daddy said between gritted teeth.

"Escort yourself or be escorted," the judge replied.

My mother stood with him and put a hand on his elbow. It shocked me when he wrenched away from her touch. They'd raised their voices over the years. One memorable Thanksgiving, Daddy even threw his baseball hat. But I'd never seen him pull away from her, not once. Stalking outside, Daddy threw a last, ugly look back. I didn't know who it was for exactly.

All I knew was that it wasn't for me.

SIXTEEN

Grey

What's most curious is that I have no idea where to start. The room she left behind should be full of clues.

I sit on the foot of the bed and ponder it like a puzzle. The family pictures are a lie. The brother is dead, one silver light in a jar that counts toward my tally. The boat is her father's. The oars belong to no vessel; the witch balls are empty magic.

Willa doesn't believe in magic. She accepts that I exist and disdains it at the same time. Now she disdains me; in this very room she believed the worst of me. I want her to take my place; my hands tremble to cover hers, and I want to breathe this curse into her mouth, feel my life come back on the warmth of her lips.

But willingly! Knowingly! I'm a creature, but not a beast. She doesn't know the difference. I admit, I'm wounded, the smallest part. I put a ripple in her still pond. She put a pea beneath my mattress.

Slipping back on my elbows, I melt into her bed. It smells of her, but only faintly. Not enough to start that pang in my chest again. I stare into the net of her canopy. Bleached shells and sand dollars dot the lines, oceanic constellations to replace the stars. Everything is the sea: her photos, her memories — but I don't think it signifies the same things to us.

My father's boat was a hateful thing to me. Cutting ice is nearly as exciting as eating oatmeal. Our path varied only by the season — to Maine in the winter, to Nova Scotia in the summer. The cold and the slick pervaded the ship. I was never warm or dry, except in my thoughts.

Boats took me nowhere, again and again. The water was lonely. Blank and bare. No better than sitting in an empty room, without even a book for company.

Throwing my arm over my eyes, I hold my breath. My sea is not Willa's sea. When I open my eyes, I intend to see it her way. I'll let myself burn and feel a taste of desperation. She did last night; she coughed and struggled, even in her senselessness.

Now, it's true I can't die. My body's not a real thing, but it plays the part beautifully. My imaginary whiskers grow. My wisplike hair falls in my eyes. An empty expanse imitates hunger. This insubstantial brain roils and sometimes has nightmares. The heart beats. It's disconnected to me, but I think I feel it all the same.

So I sit up and try to see Willa's room anew. She's here, in the whites and blues and greens. The water, the photos. But I come back to the witch balls. They quiver in the window, put in motion by an ever-shifting earth. The vibrations break the light that shines through the glass. Rays flicker along the walls, dazzling and dancing. When sunlight plays the waves, it looks much the same.

That's the answer, I decide. It's not that she bears some secret well of magic. I remain her irritating exception.

Satisfied I've unlocked her, I slide to my feet. No, there's no secret magic in her at all. It's only another taste of the ocean for her. She loves it so much, she brings it inside. She longs to live on it.

Perhaps that's the whole of Willa. It could be that she's not so complicated after all.

But as I descend to my kitchen and my newest music box, I'm bothered. It feels like someone is pressing a finger behind my ear. It doesn't hurt. It just lingers, coming from nothing, going nowhere. It makes me uneasy.

The brass bones of my oldest music box gleam in the light. I wished for a song to make sense of her, and this is what came with my breakfast. A clockwork I built a century ago, my very first. The parts hum when I touch them. Somehow, despite the hundreds I have, no matter the tedious hours I've spent building them, this one excites me.

Carefully, I pick up the movement and turn its key. The tinny pluck of each spike sounds on my skin. My body sings along; it mourns with the ballad. The lyrics are ghosts on a thin sheet of paper. They can float away; I already know this one. It's the song my father's piper played. An old tune; ancient even when I was alive.

My love said to me, "My mother won't mind
And my father won't slight you for your lack of kine."
Then she stepped away from me, and this she did say,
"It will not be long, love, till our wedding day."

The finger presses a little harder behind my ear. It means something.
I'll learn something. Sinking to my seat, I twist the key and play the
movement again.

SEVENTEEN

Willa

A car was a lousy place to have an argument. Well, maybe it was a good place for my parents. It sucked for me. The minute the driver's-side door closed, Daddy started. "What was that, Willa?"

"Leave her alone." Mom snapped her seat belt and pointed at the road. *Just go,* that gesture said. *Drive this car before I drive it for you.*

Dad stomped on the brake and threw it into gear. Then he backed out slow as molasses, because that's the way he always drove in town. Squealing tires and burned rubber would have been more dramatic. But you couldn't find somebody less dramatic than Daddy, really.

As he crept onto the highway, he looked at me in the rearview mirror. As if Mom hadn't just warned him off, he raised his brows expectantly. "Well?"

"You weren't there when the prosecutor came," I said.

My mother whipped her head around. "You did what you were told, so don't you worry about it."

I would have replied, but Daddy said, "What?"

"This isn't the only trial we've got to worry about." Ice slipped into my mother's voice. Not the polished, cutting kind. It was immovable frost instead. An iceberg. "She'll get her license back in a couple of years."

"Three," he said.

"Some things are more important than fishing."

Dad waited until he got up to speed before he exploded. "And what are we supposed to do for three years? I need Willa working the rail!"

A weight fell on me, but not on my shoulders. My sternum. It felt like my breastbone cracked, split like a Sunday chicken. He said that, and he meant it. It wasn't idle or angry. It was desperate. I didn't understand how this could be the same man who'd ordered me off the *Jenn-a-Lo*. And not just once.

Grabbing the back of my father's seat, I leaned forward to say something. To explain. But Mom put her hand up. It wasn't much of a screen, but it was enough to cut me off.

"We'll find the money somewhere. It's three years, not the end of the world."

"Like we found it this summer?"

Voice breaking, Mom strained against her seat belt. "We're still here, aren't we?"

"No thanks to you *or* me!"

Trapped in the back seat, listening to them get hoarse and ugly—I wanted to drip through the floorboards. The wheels wouldn't even thump over me if I was oil that melted into the asphalt.

Everything had changed and nothing had. I still wasn't the next in an unbroken line of Dixons fishing this shore. I still couldn't go out on the water. I was still the reason Levi was dead, only now I had a stupid, useless hope that I could pay penance for that.

"Will you just shut up and listen?" my mother yelled. Again. "Look at the bigger picture!"

"Here's a bigger picture! We're losing the boat. We're losing the business! Good thing the truck's paid off. We can back it into the kitchen and cook on the engine block when they cut off the power!"

Dad was used to keeping his hands on the wheel and his eyes in front of us, no matter what storm came. So he could scream at my mother and burn down Route 1 at eighty without blinking.

I pressed myself against the door. Through the window, the

world flashed. Autumn leaves blurred in long red-gold streaks, broken up by green, intruding pines. The flicker back and forth made my stomach turn. My fingers on the handle threatened to tighten.

It had been news to Dad that I was pleading guilty. It was news to me that he expected me back on the stern. And suddenly I was angry. There they were, yelling about me like I couldn't hear. I couldn't remember the last time any of us had talked. About anything.

Not that I could imagine sitting down and having a *chat* with my dad. He wasn't that man. And to be fair, I wasn't that girl. We liked silent agreement. And if we couldn't manage to agree, just plain silence was good too. Mom and Levi had talked. They had the same eyes and the same temperament.

It worked, we all worked, and now we didn't. None of the pieces fit, none of the edges matched up. Mom and Dad fought away in the front seat. I pressed myself harder into the glass.

When we rolled into Broken Tooth, I saw Seth's truck at the bait shop. Since he wasn't at the shore, maybe the Archambaults had gotten lucky and their boat had been spared too. Seth's dad sometimes ran overnight charters—to Boston, occasionally up to Halifax.

"Stop," I said. "I want to talk to Seth. I can walk home."

Mom frowned. "I don't think you . . ."

"Let me out!" I didn't mean to scream, but I did. It was a raw, ugly sound. I thought my throat might bleed, but I couldn't stop myself. "I'm done listening to this! I'm just done. Let me out!"

"You need to calm down right now," Mom shouted back.

Dad, though, he pulled up to the corner. Hitting the universal lock, he unlatched all four doors at once. I pushed mine open so hard, it bounced back and hit me, but I didn't care. I couldn't breathe, but I was *out,* into the sun and the quiet. I didn't know who I was, but I remembered who I used to be.

So would Seth.

"I feel bad," Seth said. "We should be down there helping."

We sat on the tailgate of his truck, at the farthest end of Stickels Cove Road. Pines closed around us, shielding us from the cool wind that came in with sunset. From our cliff perch, we watched Broken Tooth cleaning up after the storm.

Wounded boats rolled out of the water on flatbed trailers. A few had been righted and found seaworthy. Piles of broken wood and garbage rose at either end of the wharf. The *Jenn-a-Lo* bobbed at her slip, unharmed.

Peeling the label off my Moxie bottle, I nodded. Instead of untangling that rat's nest of loose traps down there, I drank bitter soda with my ex-boyfriend. I put my drink aside and leaned forward. It was a long way down to the water; it made me dizzy to look over the side.

"I know. Why aren't we?" I asked.

"Because we suck."

The light falling on us was blazing sunset, and he blazed with it. I remembered when he lost his front teeth, and the big old Chiclets that grew in the gaps. How his pug nose was too wide and too blunt in middle school. Time had stretched him out. He grew into the teeth and the nose, and an old ember warmed me. I remembered why we'd had plans.

"Don't we, though?" I said.

Seth finished his bottle and tossed it into the bin by his cab. Then he lay back in shadow to stare at the sky. "They took your license, huh?"

"Sure did."

"Wish they'd take mine," he said.

Another revelation on a day full of them. Twisting to face him, I couldn't hide my surprise. "Are you serious?"

"As a heart attack."

He plucked the sleeve of my dress, familiar, bothering. He kept doing it, until I finally stretched out beside him. Even through his jacket, I felt his heat. For the first time in a long time, I noticed the scent of his skin.

Bumping my knuckles against his, I asked, "What happened to running charters?"

"I'm sick of doing the same thing over and over."

I smiled faintly. "And the choir says amen."

"I'm serious, though, Willa." He furrowed his brow, idly hooking his finger in mine. "Aren't you?"

"I'm just tired."

"I thought everything was perfect. It wasn't. I mean, don't get me wrong. It wasn't bad. That ain't the same thing as perfect."

There was a reason Levi had always written their song lyrics. Still, the sentiment was right. It was there. Sometimes we traded who was trying too hard and who cared too much. Half the time, we overthought it, acting grown and married and forgetting to just be. To have fun. To be in love.

Winding my fingers in his, I looked over. The sun had shifted. A crimson streak of light banded his forehead. He looked ancient, and beautiful. Swallowing hard, I bumped against him. "Can I ask you something?"

"Go for it."

"Did you buy me a ring?"

Seth was quiet a long time. He seemed thoughtful, not afraid to answer the question. More like he wanted to get it right. Tightening his fingers in mine, he finally murmured, "Yeah, but I took it back."

"Well, I didn't think you—"

"The day after I bought it. Before we, before this . . ."

And yes, that stung. But at the same time, it let me breathe.

Nothing had been wrong with us; a lot of things had been right. Comfortable. We were the same shortcut to the same secret place in the woods. Nothing new to discover, and we hadn't even tried. Seth had realized it too. Maybe even realized it first.

"You should go to New York," I said. It wasn't comfortable, but I rolled onto my side. Propping my head in one hand, I dropped the other on his chest. "Make music. You used to talk about it."

"The band's gone," Seth said.

"A lot of things are gone. Apparently we're supposed to keep on living. That's what everybody's telling me."

"We miss him too, you know."

"I'm not talking about Levi tonight." I meant it. It felt a little wrong to say so. To deliberately put him in a box and put him away, but I hadn't lied. I *was* tired. Shifting to lay my head on Seth's shoulder, I pressed one finger after another into his chest. "I want you to be happy. I also wanna know what you and my dad got into it about."

With a snort, Seth sighed. "Don't you know? I'm a damned fool for breaking your heart."

I went hot all over. "I'm sorry; I didn't put him up to it."

"Didn't think you did," Seth said. "Everybody's worried, though. Where have you been lately?"

"Court. Hell. Jackson's Rock," I said.

"Bull," he replied.

"You'd think. It's true, though." I raised my head, peering at the Rock in the distance. Grey was in there somewhere, if he was real at all. Despite everything, it was still easy to disbelieve him when I was on the mainland. "I sailed right up to the back door."

"You can't. All those endangered birds." Seth raised a hand to rub his temple. Distracted, his blue eyes went blank a moment. Then he said, "I'm taking Kayla to the formal."

That was his cousin, and that fact came out of nowhere. I watched his face curiously. "Not Denny?"

Slowly pushing himself up, Seth shook his head. "No. It wasn't anything. I told you that."

"No point in wasting the tickets, I guess." I shrugged. "I'll probably go to the lighthouse just to get out of town."

"Nobody goes there. It's automatic." Seth grimaced, pressing two fingers to his temple. Then he blanked and veered again. "It was a good thing Dad was down at Peak's Island last night. He says it was smooth water and clear skies thataways."

A shiver ran through me. My gaze strayed toward Jackson's Rock. The lighthouse was nothing but a shadow on a darkening horizon. The timer hadn't gone off yet; the beacon was still. Nudging Seth, I slid to the end of the tailgate. Then, carefully, I said, "Come with me, I'll show you the island."

This time, Seth groaned. He didn't follow me to his feet. Instead, he pinched the bridge of his nose. There was no blankness, but some of his color drained away. He looked like death. "My head's killing me. Mom's probably holding dinner for me too."

"Seth," I said. I stepped in front of him, touching his chin. For a moment, I wanted to kiss him. I wanted to climb into his arms and under his clothes. He was the shortcut I knew, to a place I'd already been, but sometimes that was a good thing. Instead I glanced over my shoulder. "Let's go to Jackson's Rock."

"I could go to Seattle. I still want to be close to the water, you know? I could take my guitar and sit on the corner and play for change."

He couldn't do it. He couldn't talk about the lighthouse or the island. Realization filled me, suddenly, almost painfully.

My memories were full of blanks and headaches too. I couldn't think of anybody from Broken Tooth who had ever gone to the Rock. Plenty of people camped on other islands nearby, had parties there, bonfires . . . but never on Jackson's Rock. My head used to ache when I thought about the lighthouse. Bailey's, too; everybody's.

The island really did want us to look away.

SEVENTEEN

Grey

I'm ready. Everything is ready. I climb to the lantern gallery just as the beacon switches on for the night. The gears grind, the light hums. It charges the air, not quite like lightning, but full of portent all the same.

The tune from the music box keeps winding in my head. It seems a sign. I'm ready for Willa; she's ready for me. I'm certain, because she's thinking of me again. Though I look to the glow of souls all along the shore, all of them out of my reach, there's only one that looks back.

My anger is shed. My frustration. I'm not Susannah and Willa is not me. I have nothing to tempt her, nothing to recommend myself. But I master the sea. I stand above it, timeless, immortal. I never leave it, and it never leaves me.

This curse will not be a curse for her. It's her dream. She won't suffer the solitude of the waves. She'll embrace it. I have all of this for her. The ocean, eternal. It will always be hers; she's longed for this magic. Today and a thousand days from today, she will be the Grey Lady, and she will savor it.

There's no one to hear me, so I laugh. I lean into the wind and let the ribbon slip from my hair. My heart opens and beats; I'm exposed to moonlight and the rush of surf all around me. Soon I'll walk on that side of the water again. I'll see faces, hear voices, cut myself shaving. I haven't bled for a hundred years, and I never would have imagined this: I'm looking forward to it.

I am.

To pain and pleasure, to soup sometimes too hot. To nights sometimes too cold. To breathing. To a body that's fully real, subject to time and injury and whim. This strange almost-life that I have doesn't suit me at all. But Willa's made for it. She'll flourish in it. Just her and the water and all the time in the world.

That's all she wants. It's evident now. Her room is untouched, just as she left it. Nets for a canopy, boats for decoration. Shutters thrown open to the sea, and the slightest bit of magic hanging in the window, incongruous with the rest. There she is, solved and neat. Her destiny in a little turret chamber, her truest heart revealed.

"Come, Willa," I say.

The sound is lost in the cry of sea birds and the twist of the wind. I have no faith that she hears me, but I believe, truly believe, she feels that call. She'll come back to this island, and back to me—not with starry eyes but with purpose. I have everything she wants, and I'll give it to her. She need only ask.

EIGHTEEN

Willa

That weekend, Daddy took Mr. Eldrich out to check their pots. Because ropes get cut and accidents happen, every lobster pot has an escape hatch. Can't let ghost traps destroy the future of fishing. But that meant going out even when the fleet was turned upside down. Lobsters left in a trap too long figured out how to leave.

It also meant Mr. Eldrich and Daddy had to tell each other where they laid their trawls. It was a big thing to give up the secret, best waters they had. That's all they really had in the world. But they didn't have a choice.

Me, I stayed onshore with Bailey, untangling the traps thrown free during the storm. It was like the bottom drawer of a giant jewelry box. Ropes and loops and wire knotted together, all different colors, belonging to different boats.

"It's supposed to get cold this week," Bailey said.

She hefted a pink-painted trap over her head. Those belonged to Lane Wallace; he said it kept people from stealing them. He was wrong, though. He lost one or two to the summer jerks every year because they thought a pink lobster trap was funny.

Tugging the wrist of my glove tighter with my teeth, I plunged my hand into a nest of rope. "Maybe we should have a bonfire."

Bailey leaned her head back, letting the wind push her hair from her face. "Yeah, we could. I'm going to Milbridge later. I'll say something to Cait."

"Things better?"

"Kind of the same." Bailey stacked the pink trap with its brothers, then came back to the pile. She had swift fingers, good for working tricky wire free. She should have taken Mrs. Baxter's class. "We're going to visit her uncle Dalton later."

"The rum-smelling guy? Why?"

Rolling her eyes, Bailey shrugged. "She likes him. I don't know."

"Why are *you* go—" I cut myself off. Straightening in the tangle of rope, I tugged at my collar to let some air in. "Never mind. Stupid question."

Though I'd answered it myself, Bailey threw up her hands. "It's like we're in a play now. We both know how it ends, but we're saying all the lines and doing all the scenes anyway."

I couldn't make it better. I just knew exactly what she meant. Softly, I said, "Everything ends, Bay. Life ends. You still keep living it."

Bailey made a face. She probably would have flipped me off if her hands had been free. "Hypocrite advice, fifty cents?"

"*Experience* advice," I countered.

"Whatever." Bailey pushed on, lifting another trap from the mess and balancing it against her hip. "I'm driving. You should come with."

"Tonight?"

"Yeah, why not? Uncle Dalton's kinda woo-woo, but he's all right. Since you're all on a kick, maybe you can ask him about the Grey Lady."

"I'm not on a kick," I said. Then I added sullenly, "It's a Grey Man now."

"Not the way he tells it." Bailey added another trap to the stack, then turned to lean against it. "Just come and run interference, all right? You don't have anything better to do."

Rasping my leather glove against my brow, I marveled at her. "Seriously?"

"It's my job to call you on your shit," Bailey replied. Then she smiled, putting her head down as she reached into the pile again.

It *had* been hypocrite advice. Because as I watched my best friend work another trap free, all I could see was the space she'd leave behind. College was coming; her life far from here was already starting. In a hard way, giving up her high school sweet-heart.

And me. She had to. She'd come back for Christmas and sum-mers, we'd e-mail and call. But it wouldn't be the same. There would be somebody else to hear her everyday problems. An-other place that she called home.

Screw it, I thought. Forcing my fingers into a knot, I kicked a loose shrimp tray in Bailey's direction. "So what do I wear to a hot date with Uncle Dalton?"

I wore blue jeans and a white T-shirt. And my best fake smile, because things were worse between Cait and Bailey than maybe they even knew. They really *were* just going through the lines. They laughed in the right places; they held hands auto-matically. But the softness was gone, the dew eyes and the long looks.

So I made conversation in the truck. I talked about a bonfire we hadn't planned yet. The formal, even though I wasn't go-ing. They had dresses already, so that was a good half hour right there. When that started to die, I told them about Seth taking his cousin. That was worth another twenty minutes, and finally, we were there.

The sign said LOCKWOOD VILLAGE, but it was just one building.

A little lawn in the front, and I hoped more in the back. It smelled like baked cod and menthol in the front lobby.

Somebody played a piano, and a lot of people were scattered through the rooms. Some played cards; two watery old women faced off over a chessboard. From the looks of them, I wasn't sure they wouldn't shed blood over a checkmate.

"Hi, Uncle Dalton," Cait said. She led us to a window seat by the fireplace. It wasn't burning. I longed to get down in there and get some embers going. I sat instead, because I was running interference.

Uncle Dalton was made of paper. His hair and lips and skin were all the same dusty shade of pale. His eyes were just barely blue; only enough color to keep them from being eerie. But he smiled when he saw Cait, and patted his knee like he expected her to sit in his lap. Apparently, that was a joke, because they both laughed.

"Maybe next time," Cait said.

Undeterred, he asked, "What about you, Bailey?"

Bailey sank to sit on the floor by his chair instead. Holding up a hand, she said, "Next time, for sure."

Cait put her arm around her uncle's shoulders and nodded toward me. "I hope it's okay, we brought a friend."

"Is she pretty?" Uncle Dalton asked. Slowly, he trained his gaze on me, then offered his hand. "I guess you are. Dalton Bowker."

It made me nervous, but I shook his hand anyway. I was afraid I'd break him, but he still had strength left in his grip. He held my gaze when I replied, "Willa Dixon. It's nice to meet you."

"She lives in Broken Tooth like Bailey," Cait said.

Reclaiming his hand, Uncle Dalton leaned back in his chair. "Haven't been there for years. Zeke Pomroy still fishing out that way?"

I shook my head. Mr. Pomroy died a couple summers back, and he hadn't been out for years. It was probably tacky to tell a man as old as Uncle Dalton that somebody he remembered as living was dead, so I didn't. "His granddaughter has the boat now. Zoe. Everybody says she looks just like him."

Uncle Dalton nodded. "Better him than the wife. That woman fell out of the ugly tree and hit every branch on the way down."

Fussing even though there was nothing to fuss over, Cait kept touching his chair. The armrests, the back of it. It was like she wanted to do something to make him more comfortable, but he was fine. Sitting finally, she settled for patting his hand. "So, Uncle Dalton. I told Bailey and Willa about how you saw the Grey Lady once."

"Not me," Uncle Dalton said. "My cousin Roy. The Grey Lady was gone by the time I was born."

Tightening on myself, I curled my toes in my sneakers. Grey had said he had a predecessor. A woman. Uneasy, I folded my hands in my lap and said nothing. Since I kept my tongue, Bailey helpfully filled in for me. "Gone how?"

"Replaced." Uncle Dalton stretched, then leaned his head against the back of the chair. He looked up, not at anything. Past it. There was a sharpening in his eyes, but not for us.

"You don't have to talk about it if you don't want to," Cait said.

Brushing her off, Uncle Dalton went on. "The Grey Lady, she used to stand on the cliff and let her hair down. That's what Roy said, anyway. Nobody else saw her. Girlies, that place was abandoned even then. Gives me a headache just thinking about it."

Cold drifted over me. The divide I had, between real and Grey, wasn't so clear anymore. Not so sharp. More and more of his world slipped into mine, and it frightened me. As if I could change a story that was written before I was born, I offered, "Maybe he was just seeing things?"

Uncle Dalton wagged a finger. "My pa said Roy was a bubble off plumb. But I believed him. He meant every bit of that story, down to his blood and marrow. Cait!"

She leaned forward, attentive.

Talking right to Cait, Uncle Dalton said, "He got drunk as a skunk at my thirteenth birthday party and sat me down. Said he'd been in love with a girl named Susannah once, but he had to give her up. That she was poison, and some women were."

Maybe aware he was telling this story to three girls, Uncle Dalton looked apologetic. "He was just warning me to keep my eyes open. 'Course, I wasn't concerned about women, even then."

Cait smiled, and poked him gently. "I'm not seeing how these stories go together."

"Aren't you listening, Toots?"

Strangling a laugh, Bailey traded a look with Cait. For a second, they forgot everything was tense. They were there, again, looking into each other like nobody else existed.

Since they wouldn't, I said, "We're listening."

"She called him out to the island," Uncle Dalton said impatiently. "She asked him if he loved her, and he said yes. Then she asked if he would die for her, and he said not ripping likely, lady. Hightailed it right back to the mainland and never stepped foot in a boat again."

The first rational thing about the island or the Grey Lady I'd ever heard. With I smile, I pointed out, "Not much of a romance."

"Nothing romantic about dying. Romeo and Juliet were idiots, if you ask me."

Her coconspirator again, Bailey murmured to Cait, "I want that on a T-shirt."

Uncle Dalton shifted, his expression softening. Coming back

from whatever place he'd just been in, he sighed. "The next summer, a fella from Boston came through on an ice cutter. Then, one day, he disappeared, and up on the Rock there's a Grey Man instead of a Grey Lady."

My smile died a little. "What?"

"You heard me," Uncle Dalton said. "Don't you know the story? You get the Grey Lady on your side, and you'll have anything you wish for. But you have to trade everything you have to get it. Guess he took that deal, didn't he?"

That wasn't the story I knew. Ours was bits and pieces. Only the superstition. There were no trades in our version. No exchanges. It was just good fishing, and a faery ally in a lighthouse . . . that no one could think about for long. The wind outside whispered through the trees, but inside my skin, it howled.

Unfolding myself, I asked, "So he took her place? What happened to her?"

"Roy says he saw Susannah in town, one more time. At least, he thought it was her. The opposite of a ghost, because she had black hair and a yellow dress. She looked at Roy like she knew him, then ran out of the store. All gone, never heard from again."

Bailey leaned her head against Cait's knee. Her brows knit, she changed the subject gently. "Roy found somebody else, though, right?"

"Oh, for God's sake, yes. Married Charlotte the day she

graduated from high school. Happily ever after, nobody dying."
Shaking his head a little, Uncle Dalton looked at me. "Who are
you, again?"

I thawed myself enough to answer. "Willa Dixon. Bill Dixon's
daughter."

Studying my face, he took a minute. Then finally he asked,
"Any relation to Albert?"

In 1929, William Albert Dixon carved his initials into the back
staircase at Vandenbrook. WADII, William Albert, the second.
His son was William Eugene; Bill Gene's son, William Jack. That
was my granddad, the captain of the boat when my dad still
worked the stern. I was the firstborn, so I got the name. The
legacy. The one that had just slipped away.

Not that Uncle Dalton cared. And not that I could explain it.
So I just nodded and said. "Yessir, that's my grandfather."

Sensing I was off, Bailey nudged me with her foot. "You
okay?"

"I'm gonna get some air," I said. I claimed that I would be
right back. But instead, I walked into the night; into the cold.
And I headed for the shore.

EIGHTEEN

Grey

I wasn't sure before, how Willa came to the island. I was aware when she landed. Even now, I feel her approach. The facts of it have, until now, been entirely obscured to me. This time, I watch and see a dark marvel.

The mist comes, just a fine haze. It's a veil drawn, but a thin one—admitting light and detail, making shadows of shapes in the distance. Then at once, the haze swirls, the veil parted by unseen hands.

Introduced by an ornate prow, a boat appears. Skimming across the water, it's all but silent in its approach. There are no oars, no motor. The prow barely cuts the water. Ripples roll away from it, then melt back into the black sea.

This is magic in the open; I admit, I'm entranced. It could be the very ship that carried King Arthur to Avalon for his once and future rest.

But no, in this vessel comes my salvation. My Willa, her light more formed tonight than it has ever been.

She has a body. Her hair flows over her shoulders. Her eyes are looped with dark brows; her jaw is set. It's not the intimation. There's no blurry screen between us. Even the details I took in when I rescued her, it seems they weren't entirely focused.

Here, I thought I knew all the intricacies of my curse. Even now I learn new details. That the one who will take it from me becomes real again. That I will see more than her light; I will know her flesh. Willa's face is the first I've seen since Susannah's.

I admit, I tremble. It's the ache before a meal, when it seems impossible to wait even a minute more. The night before Christmas, when it seems dawn will never break.

It occurs to me that a gentleman would meet her at the shore. The stairs shake more than ever beneath my feet. Perhaps the lighthouse falls to pieces and remakes itself for each new keeper.

It could be the case. I promised to die for Susannah, and with that kiss, everything went white. When I woke, I found myself in a bedchamber fitted with my favorite things. I was alone; she was gone.

Until that moment, I had never been inside the lighthouse. Until that moment, I had thought only that true love called me to the cliffs. All the details—the boxes that come at breakfast, the souls I tally against my curse—those were mine to puzzle out by force and wit.

Willa won't have to suffer the first years, fogged and confused. She'll know all I know before I sail away; I wonder if the boat that brings her will take me to the shore. I wonder if I can take any of the music boxes. Or perhaps my glass news box. I rather like that. I'd like to keep it.

If not, I'll muddle through somehow. My salvation is also my tragedy. Everyone I knew is dead. I have no home onshore, no family. The world has moved on in fascinating ways. From books and newspapers, I've caught glimpses of the life that waits for me. There will be so much to learn. So much to grieve.

But everything to celebrate!

The cold gathers, a misty cloak to wear as I hurry to the beach. The shadows stalk on spindling legs, flickering through the blacks and greens of the forest. Shells crackle beneath my feet. They're proof of ancient inundations; once this island was sea, and the sea, this island.

The path to the shore is direct; it crosses the second-highest point on the island. At the apex, moonlight fills the clearing. In all truth, I would dance here if I had no errand. I'd sing, old songs and new ones. I'd sing, "It will not be long, love, till our wedding day."

We'll be celebrating a different sort of marriage entirely. Joining Willa with the island, matching myself to the living, waking world.

Though I hurry, Willa's already splashing through the surf when I break into the clearing.

Willa's too impatient for the boat to land. She jumps from it, wading through knee-deep water to get to me. I falter because she's not an impression anymore.

The light that signals her life still glows, but from within a physical shape now. Like a boy, she wears trousers. Like a little girl, she lets her hair hang loose. Something silver flashes at the curve of her nose; silver crawls down the curve of her ear.

My hunger trembling has force now. If I had no control of myself, I'd leap at her. Clutch her freckled hands, press against her curls—put my mouth to hers, not for a kiss, but to draw out her breath.

Fully revealed, she's beautiful. She's alive. She's everything I want. I hold out my hands to her and start to speak. She slaps them away; she cuts me off.

"What did you do to me?" she demands.

NINETEEN

Willa

He stood there, blinking at me like he was confused. His face was so smooth, I'd mistaken it for soft. Innocent, maybe. I only waited a second. Then I asked again, jabbing a finger at him. "What did you do to me, Grey?"

"This is going to make you angry," he said, "but in what sense?"

He wasn't wrong. The way he avoided the subject plucked my last, raw nerve. I was sure he knew exactly what I meant. That he wanted me to drag it out so he could keep me here longer. The only thing I didn't know for sure was why.

"In the sense of, why am I here? What is this place, exactly? What are *you?*"

Grey raised his brows. Pleasantly, he nodded. Folding his fingers together, he said, "Of course, in that sense."

"Well?"

"Will you walk with me?" He saw me shudder, so he was quick to add, "On the path alone. After last time, I think it best to stay out of the lighthouse. I never know what it might do."

Or what he might do. I looked at the forest; I'd never been afraid of it before. It wasn't my element, but it was part of my home. But now that the leaves had fallen, the bare branches were skeletal fingers, beckoning. I shook my head. "I don't want to walk with you. I want you to . . ."

He offered me his elbow. When he tipped his head to me, there was a second when I thought I saw a hazy top hat there. The shape melted, but the impression stayed. If he was gonna insist, I could go along. Just the woods. Just the path. With so many trees bare, I'd be able to see the shore. It was going to be fine.

So I put my hand on his arm, but I didn't hold it. It was enough of a gesture, because Grey finally started walking.

With an air of thoughtfulness, he was quiet a minute. Then he said, like he was explaining mathematics, "I'm the Grey Man."

"That part I know." I led him to the forest path. The one with tiny seashells scattered beneath the trees. They sounded like shattering glass under my boots. "You get presents at breakfast, you can't leave, I get all that. Why? Why any of this?"

Grey turned a long, slow look on me. "There's magic involved. You can have anything you want, but you're charged to be the sentinel in the lighthouse."

"I didn't ask for a speech, Shakespeare."

"I'm explaining it the best I can. I was tricked into taking the position, so it's been a challenge to work it out on my own. This lighthouse is my post; I choose how to administer it. I can call the fog or send it away, and I, Willa, have spent a hundred years driving it away. I have no dominion over the tides or the winds, the storms or the snow. But I can smother this world if I choose."

Over and over in my head, I told myself to just go with it. Whatever rules there were on the mainland, in the real world, they didn't apply here. If he said he was the north wind and Santa Claus combined, I was gonna believe it, for as long as I had to. So instead of calling him a liar, I said, "And you're not the first."

"Alas, one of many." He gestured vaguely at himself. "The latest in a long line of sentinels. I only know what came to me when I woke to it, and I've told you, that was a century past."

Narrowing my eyes, I said, "How many, then? How long has there been a *sentinel*?"

Grey shrugged. "Ages. Before there was a lighthouse. I think one of the others must have wished for that. Alas, I asked for a full and true accounting of every Grey to stand the post. It was the one thing that never appeared wrapped in ribbon at my plate. Perhaps it's an old Indian curse."

"Yeah, I'm pretty sure if the Passamaquoddy had magic like that, neither one of us would be standing here."

Touching fingers to his chest, Grey said, "'There are more things in heaven and earth, Horatio.'"

The pines creaked around us, laughing. Their needles fell on bare granite, and I stiffened. It felt like Grey was talking down to me. Calling me stupid. Maybe a slap back for calling him Shakespeare. I didn't like it, so I pushed him to get to the point.

"That's real helpful."

Like he was placating me, Grey reached for me. Then he curled his fingers back at the last moment, taking his touch away so I couldn't avoid it. "I think there's something primal about this island. Something we've never named and never known. To the beginning of humanity, perhaps."

This was going nowhere. He knew what I wanted to know, but he kept veering away from it. It could have been I was asking the wrong questions. There wasn't a guidebook for interrogating a ghost. Or a curse. Or . . . I still didn't know what he was. Since origins got me nowhere, I tried another way of asking.

"Okay, fine, there's always been a Grey on the island. Fine." My fingers tightened on his arm. "So what do you mean, you got tricked?"

Grey slowed as we approached the clearing, the highest point on the island. He let my hand slip from his elbow and turned his face to the sky. With arms spread, he turned a slow circle, his hair wisping around his shoulders.

"I was a fool. I imagined myself in love with an illusion. And like a fool, I offered myself as a sacrifice to that love."

"In English?"

The edges of Grey's manners slipped. He scowled, his black eyes cutting past me furiously. "My true love asked if I would die for her. And when I said yes, she kissed me and conferred all the glory you see before you. She walked away in her flesh and left me as nothing but mist."

The constellations shifted. I didn't notice it at first. I had more on my mind than tracking time by the skies. I forgot that time moved faster on Jackson's Rock. That a cup of cocoa could pass an entire day. The forest darkened around us, lights twinkling above as the cold came in.

Wrapping my arms around myself, I circled the edge of the clearing. I didn't want to sit down with him. Get comfortable. Forget that I came for a reason. Stopping against the shadow of a great oak, I asked, "Why am I the only one who can think about Jackson's Rock without getting a splitting headache? Why am I the only one who can come here?"

Grey's hesitation wasn't uncertainty. The answer seemed to fly to his lips. But he held it there, and I wasn't sure why. When he said it, he spoke carefully. Like he was afraid he would say it too fast and it would dissipate. "You've been chosen. I think; I believe this: you came here because you wanted an escape."

"Excuse me?"

Warming, Grey approached. His fingers fluttered when he talked; the tips of them evaporated into faint contrails. "The night I pulled you from the water! You couldn't leave because there was something you didn't want to face on the shore. In your heart, you wanted to stay!"

My court date, I thought. Out loud, I said, "I don't think so."

"This place, this . . . gift. It's everything you've ever wanted, Willa. You love the sea. You love these waters. Not just any beach. Not just any cliff. This place, it's your legacy. And it could be yours eternally. You could be the Grey Lady. The one who steers the ships home. Or keeps them in the harbor when a storm is coming. You wouldn't be one girl here for one short lifetime. You'd be greater than your flesh. Mistress of the light, and the lives onshore."

Silence fell in the forest. Even the wind stilled. Grey was so animated, so excited. He sounded like a brimstone preacher, believing every single word of his gospel. Uneasy, I considered him. Then I asked, "Why would you think that?"

"You told me!" He pointed at the lighthouse. "Your room

there, it told me everything. The witch balls in the window—you've been longing for a little magic in your life, Willa. And all the rest is the sea. I can give you that."

My mouth dropped open. That's how he'd figured it? With a disbelieving laugh, I told him, "Witch balls turn away the evil eye. Like the glass beads in old nets. They're not about wanting magic. They're supposed to keep it away."

Grey's face fell. "But this is your destiny."

"Yeah, no, it's not." Pushing off the tree, I met him in the middle. "I lost my brother this summer—I told you that. You really think I *want* to walk away from the rest of my family? From my friends? It's been a lousy couple of months, but no. Just no."

Confused, Grey pulled a tiny box from his pocket. It was silver, blue glass laid into its sides. When he turned the key, plaintive notes trickled out. They twisted on a new wind. Each note echoed in its own way; it took me a minute to recognize the tune.

When the fishing was good, Daddy sometimes got on the radio and sang. Just a verse or two—a dirty song about ruffles and tuffles sometimes. Chanteys sometimes. But usually this song. "She Moved Through the Fair," slow and haunting and dark.

Shining with a light I'd never seen before, Grey smiled when the song wound down. The last note plucked, and he offered me the box. "I wished for something to make sense of you, and this is what I got. It's a message."

"You know that song, Grey?"

"I've heard it many times."

"Yeah, but do you *know* it?" I asked.

The expression drained from his face. "Do you?"

Fear crept through me because I knew something Grey didn't. I knew all the words; I'd heard the song a hundred times. Uneasy, I glanced back to make sure the dory waited for me at the shore.

Then, I turned to him and said, "She never comes back, Grey. He sees her once at the fair and spends the rest of his life missing her."

If it was possible, Grey paled. Closing the box in his hand, he stiffened. "She whispers in his dreams."

"It's all in his head." Though my heart pounded, I went on. "Whatever magic that works here, whatever gave you that music box? It wasn't wrong. Because I'm not your escape."

He broke. I saw it in his eyes. In the trembling of his hands. It was like he'd been sleeping two sleeps, one of curses and one of fantasies. I'd just shattered the only beautiful one for him.

When he said nothing, I moved toward the path. Still he said nothing, and panic bloomed in me. Until now, he'd never been at a loss for words. If some terrible, devil version of him existed, I didn't want to see it.

When my feet hit the path, he screamed. A plaintive wail, one that echoed longer than it had lasted. Then he called after me.

"Don't go! I'm alone. I'm going mad; it'll take thousands of years to collect enough souls to get off this island!"

It felt like he'd thrown a spear. Like I'd been split and pinned by it. My chest hurt, and my head, too. I *knew* there had to be something else. There had to be something he'd been sugarcoating. "Souls?"

"I'm not a monster," he raged. "I could have smothered your village's fleet a hundred times by *now*. Lost them all at sea, collected every soul at once, and I never have! I've been a boon to Broken Tooth. I've kept you all safe! Kept you safe in particular, Willa. The night you and your brother went into the dark, I tried to protect you. To hide you!"

"What do you mean?"

"Come with me," he said. He held out a hand. It was pale, and in the moonlight, it looked skeletal. Suddenly, he was a long, gangling thing. Bones and angles, and it made my skin crawl. But I followed him, because I had to know. Because he had something inside his head, and it had to do with me, and Levi, and I had to know.

It wasn't the music-box room when we went through the door of the lighthouse this time. Not the kitchen, either, or any of the rooms I'd seen. It looked like a pantry, sort of. Wood doors lined the walls. A bitter smell wafted on the air, like old paper, or an unused closet. Grey opened one of the doors.

Row after row of glass bottles lined the inside. Each hung in its own nook. Corked, they were empty. And they didn't make sense. The jars weren't much bigger than my thumb. They didn't look like test tubes or like they were for spices. Light reflected on their rounded bottoms. I tightened my arms around myself because a chill came on.

"I could have collected you the night of the storm," Grey said. "I risked myself. I tore myself to shreds to get to you, to save you! I am *not* a monster."

The jars *tink*ed, shaking in their neat slots. It was like they were alive. Or something bigger than all of us was subtly shaking the lighthouse. My heart decided to quiver too. I felt sick and uneasy, but all I could do was ask questions.

"How's that, Grey? It doesn't even make sense."

Closing one door, Grey opened another. Tilting his head to the side, like he was admiring art, he considered the three uppermost jars. They glowed, like each one had a firefly caught inside. When I stepped closer, Grey pressed himself between me and his precious jars.

"There are two ways off this island. The first? Collect a thousand souls. Anyone who dies on the water, beneath my light . . . a tally in my book. This is a century's worth."

All my blood drained away. I felt raw and cored, and I wanted to fall to my knees. If this was the truth, if any of it was real . . .

My head split; it felt like Grey had dropped an axe instead of some words. Too many questions. Too many possibilities.

My hand shaking, I pointed. "What is that?"

"All that remains."

I lunged past him, trying to grab the bottle. It was like hitting a wall. Icy, immovable. When I lunged again, the pantry shifted. It was there, then I took a breath, and it was gone. All that was left was music boxes. All of them, keys ticking. Notes playing. Each one played a different song, none of them in tune. In time.

Throwing myself at Grey, I grabbed his shirt. I shook him. "You let my brother die!"

"No, Willa," he said, newly, coldly calm. "You killed your brother. I only kept what was mine."

I tasted bile, but I wasn't gonna turn myself inside out for Grey. For that *thing*. For all I knew, it was a hallucination. Another lie. There was nothing left of Levi. He was dead and gone. *Gone.*

Shells and stones ground beneath my feet, because I walked away. I *ran*. Putting my back to him, to that lighthouse, I dared him to do something about it. I wasn't gonna be a part of this. Everything on the Rock would become myth again for me, I hoped forever.

"I promised to be honest with you, Willa! You can't hold the truth against me. Your brother was one more toward a thousand, it's true! But he was a happy accident. One I tried to prevent, one you engineered!"

Biting my own lips, I held in a reply. I held in everything: my gaze, my voice, my churning belly. If I could have made it a mile in icy water, I would have swum home instead of getting into that cursed boat.

Instead, I sat at the bow, staring into the sea. Staring at the shore. Looking everywhere but behind me.

I was never going back to Jackson's Rock, not even with my eyes.

NINETEEN

Grey

When the Big Dipper is upside down, it will rain for three days.

My father believed that—he, long dead now. My mother didn't; she, too, molders in the earth. Every home I ever knew is ashes. Every street I ever walked, paved over. No one I knew by name, who could greet me with mine, remains aboveground.

The stars are all turned, and it hasn't stopped raining since Willa left. Cold, ice rain that makes me glad I only imagine my body. I think I save myself from the worst of mundane realities. I feel cold, but I don't go numb with it. I feel heat, but I never sweat.

Because I'm dead. A remnant. A revenant.

She's not thinking of me.

I'll never be free.

TWENTY

Willa

Every time I started to look toward the Rock, I distracted myself. It was hard, because the weather went crazy. Well, not the weather so much. The fog.

It rolled in and out, wildly random. The horn blared constantly, sometimes for ten minutes, sometimes for four hours. It was like a strobe light in slow motion. White, then clear. Clear, then white.

But distraction didn't come too hard. The way my parents saw it, I'd disappeared for three days after court. Long enough that they reported me missing. Long enough that a patrol car came to our house when I turned up.

I sat in the living room. Head hanging, I suffered through the lecture Scott Washburn gave me. He talked like I was supposed to forget he was my lazy-eyed cousin just because he was wearing a badge.

"That kind of irresponsible behavior, you set people to worrying," Scott said. "There's been enough trouble in Broken Tooth this year, don't you think?"

Stepping on my own toes, I didn't even lift my head. "I know. I said I was sorry."

With a suddenly sympathetic face, Scott stared at me real hard. "Where have you been? You in some kind of trouble?"

"I've been around."

Dad made a disgusted sound. My mother echoed him with irritated precision. "Around."

"I haven't been fishing, if that's what you want to know."

"You're just making this hard on yourself," Scott said.

"I hear that a lot," I snapped. Cutting a look at my parents, I spread my hands. "I hid out in Uncle Toby's cabin, all right? It was quiet. I wanted some time to think."

They all relaxed. That's why it was a perfect lie. Uncle Toby's cabin was an old hunting lodge up in the woods. Surrounded by blueberry barrens, hidden in the trees—it had been abandoned in the fifties. We all sort of owned it, and most everybody in Broken Tooth had spent a night or two there. It was full of graffiti and other people's first times.

"That place is dangerous." Scott had to say it; nobody believed it.

I apologized, and they didn't have to know I wasn't sorry. I hadn't meant to disappear like that. Time on the Rock was different. Somehow I forgot that at the worst possible moment. I wondered if I was three days older. If my molecules had kept the time, or if I was just stopped when I was there.

A real important question Grey needed to answer, since he wanted off that rock so bad. He might be happy to stay there if he knew he'd crumble to a hundred and seventeen years' worth of dust if he left.

"Am I dismissed?" I asked, because I wasn't thinking about Grey. I wanted to get out of the house.

Scott shrugged at my parents. Mom stepped right in; at least she was a warden I was used to. "You're leaving this house to go to school and back, period. I'll walk you if I have to. This nonsense stops today."

I shrugged. "Okay."

Since they didn't know what to do with compliance, Mom and Dad fell quiet. Since Scott was her side of the family, Mom followed him to his car and saw him off. Daddy pushed the curtains back. He watched her stop on the walk to talk with Scott, then finally turned to me.

"I figured you needed a year off."

Though I knew he was talking to me, I guess it didn't sink in exactly. It was so unexpected, I didn't know what to do. I stared up and realized he'd gotten so old. Not just the grey in his hair or the lines in his face. He seemed shorter, shoulders slanted. His cheeks were hollower. The circles under his eyes deeper. And his voice was soft, gruff, as he sat in the rocker by the window.

"Didn't intend for you to stay off the boat forever," he said. "I figured, come next summer, you'd be all right."

Unsure what he meant, I leaned forward. "Daddy, I'm fine."

He waved a hand at me, brushing that claim aside like it was a black fly. "I think not. Nobody's fine. There's nothing to be fine about. It's my place to protect you. You and Levi both. I did a piss-poor job of it with Levi . . ."

An ache consumed me, and I was quick to cut him off. "It wasn't your fault, Daddy. We all know . . ."

"Look," he said. He rocked the chair forward and perched there. Hands knotted up, they flickered as he dredged up more words for me than he ever had. "You're a Dixon. We're nothing like your mother's people. You go on and take the blame, 'cause there's no getting through that hard head of yours. But I'll take it too, for the same reason. It is what it is, Willa."

My eyes burned, tears spilling over. "What are we going to do until I get my license back?"

Closing back up, Daddy let the rocker go. "I'll mind my business. You mind yours."

"Daddy."

"I expect you to graduate on time." Tugging a cap over his eyes, he pretended that he was going to nap. "So you've got a whole lot of work to make up."

He faked drifting off just in time for my mother to sweep back into the house. She slammed the door and cut me with a look. Then, because she apparently thought just sitting there wasn't punishment enough, she pointed at the kitchen.

"You get in there and do the dishes. I'm too mad to look at you."

Peeling myself from the couch, I made my way to the kitchen. And though I didn't have Levi to rinse or to elbow me or to squeeze the soap bottle until tiny bubbles floated around our heads, things in my house felt almost normal. Not quite settled, but heading that way.

They weren't.

Music blared from my computer, and Bailey's notebooks covered my bed.

It was kind of terrifying how much junk she kept stuffed in her backpack. She took beastly notes for every class, wrote down every assignment, knew when everything was due.

Basically, she treated school like a contact sport, and by God, she was gonna win at it. All that organization was good for her scholarship prospects. And good for me, trying to figure out if I'd accomplished anything since the first day of classes.

"I know you didn't do this," Bailey said. She spread a photocopied sheet in front of me. "Because it's group work, and I know how you are."

Cussing under my breath, I looked over the requirements. "Well, I can't do it now."

"Just finish it yourself."

Rolling my eyes at her, I put that sheet aside. "Uh huh."

"You're grounded," Bailey said. She snatched the page up and flattened it in front of me again. "You don't have anything better to do. And in case you forgot? I'm the boss of you."

She was. Mom set Bailey loose, invested her with homework superpowers or something. If I wanted to do anything besides stare at my own bedroom walls, I had to let Bailey work me like a sled dog. It was a job she relished—so much that I was finally sorry for cutting all those days.

Turning herself in circles, Bailey suddenly produced a fan of assignments. "These are the easy ones. Do them first to get some momentum."

"They're essays," I said, miserable.

"Exactly. I'm holding back the research report you have to do for Econ."

Sliding to the floor, I groaned. I'd get it all done because I had to. But I wasn't gonna like it. Not even a little bit. With a flick through the essay assignments, I rearranged them from easy to hard. Then I held them up for Bailey's inspection. "Well?"

"I see sirens," Bailey answered nonsensically.

Red and blue lights flashed outside. No matter how many times Seth argued that the lights were *silent*, Bailey still called them sirens.

We stepped over notebooks to get to my window. It was the second time that week that a cop had been at my door. This time, it didn't seem to be for me.

My cousin Scott stood on the porch, and my parents went outside. Bailey pulled my blinds, and I lifted the window as quietly as I could. Though the lights made no noise, the patrol car's idling engine did. It was hard to pick out words; whole sentences came out garbled.

Bailey leaned her head against mine and whispered. "I think he said the case is going?"

"Going where?" Neither of us knew, and we weren't even sure that's what he really said. I pressed against the screen. Its dusty weave made me wheeze, but I held my cough.

"What?" my mom barked.

That rang out, clear and pure. But what followed didn't. Frustrated, I closed the window. Gesturing at the stairs, I said, "I'm just gonna go ask."

"You have work to do," Bailey said. As if she hadn't just been pressed to the window with me.

She only said it to prove she was trying to do her job. It didn't stop her from scrambling after me. Since it was probably family business, she stopped at the top stair. I went down first, Bailey right behind me, to wait for Mom and Dad to come inside.

When they did, they were fire and ice. Mom's face was scarlet, Daddy's dirty white. They shut the door with Scott still on the other side of it. Startled to see me, Dad shook his head and set my mother's arm free. "I'll make coffee."

He passed me without a word, and my heart sank. Reaching for my mother, I asked, "What's wrong?"

"You should get back to work," she said.

I refused to move. "Mom."

"Scott's not sure," Mom said, her voice thick with judgment. "But he thinks something's going on with the grand jury."

Glancing up the stairs, I took comfort when Bailey pressed her hands to her chest. She didn't have to say anything to know exactly how I was feeling: wounded and wary and afraid. I rubbed my mother's back, like she used to rub mine when I was little and sick to my stomach. "What kind of something?"

Still furious, my mother snapped, "Like I said, Scott's not sure. He came all the way over here to stir us up because 'there's chatter.' I hear chatter all night on dispatch. There's no need to run over, lights flashing, for *chatter*."

"There's nothing wrong, though, is there?"

Daddy emerged from the kitchen. Behind him, the coffeepot

gurgled—an ordinary sound that seemed so out of place. The house groaned, shifting beneath our feet. And in the distance, the foghorn went off again. It lowed in the dark, distant and lost.

"Bad news travels faster than good," Daddy said.

"But I'm supposed to testify." Turning between them, I couldn't tell if I was talking or begging. Panic ran through me; it stole my reason and my sense. "I was there! Doesn't that matter?"

Mom clamped a hand on my shoulder. "Willa, stop it. Until there's something to know, you need to settle down. I'm sure Bailey has better things to do than tutor you. Get on up there and quit wasting her time."

Nudging me toward the stairs, Mom waited for me to go. How she expected me to work I didn't know.

The grand jury wasn't even the trial. It was a bunch of shuffling papers and looking at evidence. The way Ms. Park explained it to me, the grand jury was there to decide if there was enough evidence to charge Terry Coyne with killing my brother.

I was there. I saw it. I felt it. I knew exactly who fired that gun. It was a damned given, so what was going wrong with the grand jury? I'd pointed out the right picture in the mug shot book. My feet pounded on the stairs. Bailey caught me by the shoulders.

"It's okay," she said. "It'll be okay."

When our eyes met, though, I knew it wasn't. Bailey was the one who had optimism on her side. Instead of certain, she looked worried. No doubt, I looked crazed. Between the two of us, I expected we had a right to be both.

TWENTY

Grey

Here I am, rampant.

I stand in the lamp gallery, a jar in hand. The light inside it doesn't glow so bright as the one that spins behind me. When I hold the jar high, it seems almost empty.

Four in a hundred years. It's an impossible task, and it always has been. Sisyphus and his rock. My humble self and these souls. I'd laugh, but nothing's funny anymore.

I keep throwing myself off the lighthouse. Again and again, I plunge into the sea. Ripped apart and reincorporated, I find the smallest pleasure in the fact that it's starting to hurt. My veins bear no blood, my flesh contains no bone. But whatever magic keeps me together, it's exhausted and aching.

The masquerade of breakfasts and dinners is over. If I were a real boy, I'd be parched. Nothing to drink for days—could be a week or more. Letting time slip away is a gift to myself. Better than music boxes or books or nonsense, all the nonsense I used to wish for.

As autumn cedes to winter, I cede to the mist.

Like a monk, I shaved my head. Like an ascetic, I stripped to the waist. No shoes, no gloves. No tie, no hair oil. Now I realize the true choice I had when I took Susannah's place. The soul collection only distracted me. It was more fundamental than that. Or should I say, more elemental.

Be human or be mist. Lure the next Grey to the island or surrender. All this time, the island knew, the lighthouse knew, that I was meant to succumb. Magic mocks me. It laughs and echoes through the trees.

The only reason Willa came was to put on a show. To delight whatever ancient god or demon that resides within this rock.

Reason tells me she was a pawn, but the elements have no reason. They're capricious and unknowable; they contain no conscience. I hate her, I curse her. I stand here at the edge of my world with her brother's soul in the palm of my hand.

I've no idea what will happen if I break the glass.

What happened when I captured him? It's a question that only now occurs to me. Did I impede his progress to heaven or hell? Do those ethereal realms even exist? This bottled light could be anything—a breath, a thought. The whole sum of a being, and I keep it in a cupboard, like last summer's jam.

Leaning over the rail, I hold the jar aloft. The lighthouse groans, the beam making another pass. When the light drowns me, I drop my prize.

My whole purpose for being. Four souls in a hundred years; now I have but three.

The sea roars, and the gears grind. Everywhere, wind swirls and whispers. These raw aspects of nature clamor; they devour the sound of glass breaking on the rocks. Avidly, I watch. But there's no light lifting ever skyward. No flicker delving into the deep. It seems—when I set free a collected soul—that nothing happens at all.

I'm disappointed.

Because I can, I call the fog until it's thick around the light. I, too, am capricious, so I banish it by sheer force of will. Then I fling myself over the side again. The sensation of gravity gives way to a sudden, concussive ache.

When I come back together, I find myself standing in front of the cupboard. My remaining three jars tremble. Pulsing with light, they seem to react to one another. And when I reach for one, the lights within them dim. Perhaps they realize what comes next.

Perhaps they realize that I'm *the monster on the rock*.

TWENTY-ONE

Willa

Because the fog was so erratic, some of the juniors started gathering the little kids in groups to guide them to the school. Parents walked their kids to the base of the hill, then we waited until we had a whole class to lead.

The heat from the path thinned the haze, giving us a clear shot from the village to the school. As long as everybody stayed on the pavement, we could get up safely and back down again at the end of the day.

Somehow, it just got organized. Seth had kindergarteners, and Bailey scored the sixth-graders. They had no trouble herding their classes to Vandenbrook.

It wasn't so easy for me. I ended up with fourth-graders. Though I couldn't prove it, I suspected their parents gave them Red Bull and straight sugar for breakfast. They were old enough that they argued about holding hands, and little enough that they could disappear in two seconds.

I lost the Lamere twins the second day and nearly had a nervous breakdown. Calling my throat raw, I scoured the path from top to bottom four times. Right when I thought I'd have to call the police, I found them. They sat on a stump just off the path, building a faery house out of shells and sticks.

After that, I made my kids say one letter of the alphabet each, in order, all the way up the hill. If a *J* or a *Q* dropped off, I knew I had a runner.

Denny streamed past with her white blond hair and an orderly line of first-graders. It wasn't until she got the whole class ahead of me that she turned around. And it unnerved me, because she met my gaze on purpose. Her face was soft, her lips pursed.

She looked thoughtful. Or sorry. Something sympathetic, and it dragged a cold touch along the nape of my neck. That wasn't the face of the girl who'd spat at my feet or gone riding with my boyfriend. I raised my hand to acknowledge her.

Fog curling around her pale head, Denny only stood there. Then, out of nowhere, she said, "I liked Levi, you know."

Stiff, I tried to nod. "There was a lot to like."

Whatever had stopped Denny pushed her to move again. She swept up her first-graders and flowed on toward school. Her voice echoed in my head. It hurt in a whole new way to hear my brother's name. Like forcing a needle through a blister and going too deep. It left me with a sour taste in my mouth.

I turned back to my fourth-graders, then heard Nick calling in the distance. It was another blister to recognize my name on his voice, actually. We hadn't talked since the bonfire; I wasn't sure I wanted to. But his little sister was in fourth grade, and she hadn't been at the base of the hill when we were ready to head up. They must have been running late together.

I put one hand on each of the twins' heads to keep them from wandering and called back, "I'm not going anywhere!"

From the pale, Nick appeared. He was shaggy as ever, clinging to his sister's hand. But instead of letting go, he plowed into my fourth-graders and pointed back to town. "Your mother's been trying to call you. She says go home right now."

My heart knotted, and I shook my head. "I can't, I've got to walk them up."

"She smells like cheese," Jamie Lamere volunteered beneath my hand.

Nick clamped him by the back of the neck and nodded me away. "I've got 'em. Seriously, Willa, you better go."

Fixed in place, I hesitated. But just for a second, only long enough to hand over Ash Lamere, too. That one thought I smelled like onions, and he wanted to start the alphabet. I thanked Nick and ducked away from them, walking just short of a run. Pulling my cell from my pocket, I shook it, like that would make it ring or something.

Suddenly, the fog burned off. Not gradually; instantly. It was so clear, I could see the church steeple at the other end of town. Completely bare, trees stretched their naked limbs, sharp, black streaks against the sky. There were no clouds, not even a contrail to break the expanse of blue. This light washed everything brighter. Cleaner.

As I turned the corner onto Thaxter Street, I slowed. An unfamiliar car sat in front of my house. Its shape nagged at me as I came up the walk. Like I should have been able to place it. Once I opened the front door, it made sense. Ms. Park, the prosecutor, stood in the middle of my living room.

She held her elbows at awkward angles. Kinda like she wanted to comfort my mother but didn't know how.

When I stepped in, she looked to me. Her smooth poker face revealed nothing, and my mother saved her the trouble of speaking.

"They're not gonna charge Terry Coyne," Mom said coldly. Blame flowed from her. She held out a hand to me, and that was soft. But her face was hard. Her eyes were diamonds, flashing from my face to Ms. Park's. "There was a problem with the *warrant*. The bullets in his car *don't count*."

Ms. Park tried to soften it. "They don't, and I'm so sorry. But this is only a setback. We're running down a lot of other evidence."

"There wasn't any," I said, lips numb.

"There's always more evidence," Ms. Park replied. She even sounded like she believed it. "And we still have you."

"Then let me talk," I said. "I saw it all. I was there. They have to listen to me."

"And they will. But you're not enough, Willa. Not for an indictment, not for a conviction. And I'd rather convict Mr. Coyne in five years than let a jury find him not guilty now."

Throat raw, I spun toward Mom, then back to Ms. Park. It didn't make sense to me. The bullets made a connection, yeah. But I'd seen it all. I was there. I could have sat in a courtroom and pointed him out all day long. For the rest of my life, I'd never forget his face in the night, and that should have counted for *everything*.

My voice broke as I insisted, "But I was *there*."

Ms. Park said something soothing and meaningless. That only ticked my mother off, and she started shouting. It was a hazy mess to me, voices tangled up. High and low, loud and soft.

When it got hot, Ms. Park said she'd come as a courtesy, that she wanted to make sure Mom heard it from *her*, and not the news. Ma told her where she could shove that courtesy.

The next thing I knew, Mom had chased the prosecutor out

of the house. I followed my mother to the porch, just in time to catch her. She didn't faint, she just gave up on standing. Flailing at the world, she didn't want to be set down gentle, but I did it anyway.

Curling around her, I tried to soak up her tears. I tried to calm her—like Ma Dyer said, I tried to help her breathe. But this was a kind of drowning nobody could save her from. Especially not me. I was going down with her. I could only manage one thought, tangled in grief with her like that.

"Does Daddy know?" I asked, rocking with her and digging my fingers in.

He didn't. Not yet. But he would.

Twisting braids into my hair, Bailey sat on the top porch step, and I sat on the bottom. Her knees framed my shoulders. With every new knot, she made my head bob. I was her marionette, and I sort of wished she could just stay in charge of me.

After the shock, all I had was despair. My legs didn't want to support my weight any more than I wanted to stand. If I had, I might have walked into town. I might have seen Terry Coyne buying a box of chew and sucking on a bottle of root beer.

Bailey dragged another lock into place. There were too many obvious things to talk about. When my father would be home (soon). How he had reacted to the news (badly). Whether Mom should have told him in person instead of over the radio (nope).

Instead, Bailey kept my buzzing head full of things that didn't matter. Mental sandbags against the coming flood. "I heard Amber was chasing Nick around, angling to get invited to the winter formal."

"Good luck with that," I said.

"I know, right?" Bailey tipped my head the other way. "Cait got her dress, did I tell you?"

"Uh-uh."

"It's blue, with silver lacy stuff on top. It matches that bracelet you made."

"Hope they sew better than I string beads."

Cranking my head all the way back, Bailey looked down at my face. "Not really. It's all ragged at the bottom, and it's only got one shoulder. It's like Picasso in real life. I'm not sure how any of the parts match up. I'm afraid too much is going to show."

Grim, I smiled. "Mean."

"Truth." Bailey let my head go, then made a soft, worried sound. "There's Dad's truck."

In a way, I expected him to screech up to the house, tires smoking and brakes protesting. Instead, the old pickup glided toward us. Smoke filtered from the window; Daddy wasn't even trying to hide his cigarettes now.

My stomach went bitter. The memory of ash in my mouth

was vivid; I felt the roll of the boat again. The ache in my head from hitting the glass—it was all brand new. One of Bailey's hard tugs brought me back to the present. Daddy pulled into the driveway, but he didn't kill the engine.

He got out and walked straight for the house. The blankness on his face matched the eerie certainty of his steps. Possessed by something, he moved slow and deliberate. I was halfway to my feet when he reached the porch, but he didn't even look at me.

Brushing past, he left the door open when he went inside. Untangling myself, I started after him. Just then, my mother cried out.

"Bill!" she shouted. "Bill, you stop it right now."

Panic rippled through the air. I burst inside, then plastered myself against the wall. Daddy dropped the stock of his shotgun against his shoulder. Buckshot shells rattled as he dropped them into his pocket.

I wanted to say something, but my throat was stuck. It was too much, everything was too much. Frozen, I ground my shoulders against the wall and watched in horror.

Putting his head down, Daddy moved like my mother wasn't tearing at his shirt. Like he didn't hear her, see me. Bailey jumped out of his way, her face drained of all color. Cracking the brittle tension, I forced myself to follow.

Our dooryard wasn't that big. Bleak, thorned rose vines clung to the gate trellis. Scattered with fallen leaves and long shadows, it looked like a cemetery. Mom dug in her heels, scattering the leaves. She tripped and hauled herself up. Wild and feral, she flung herself at Daddy.

"You can't do this, Bill," my mother sobbed.

She struggled against him, pounding his back with her fists. The blows fell away; she may as well have punched a wall. When he turned, I was afraid he would hit her. Instead, he pulled her hands off his flannel and held her at arm's length.

Behind me, Bailey chanted, "Oh God, oh God, oh God," less a prayer than an exclamation. Struggling against my reluctant body, I jumped the steps and ran toward the driveway. I reached the truck just as Daddy slammed the door closed.

He reached out the window to shove my mother away. Even in that he was gentle, but he was firm. It was terrible, a slow-motion severing.

For a second, everything seemed to float. A snapshot of a moment: my mother catching herself on the fence, my father hanging out the window. I would have sworn that time stopped —no, skipped. A blank flicker when Daddy met Mom's eyes and said, "Goodbye, baby."

Slumping on the fence, Mom started to sob. Daddy threw the truck into reverse and tore out of the driveway. When time started again, I moved with it. I ran after the truck, like I might actually catch it. Arms windmilling when I realized I couldn't, I twisted around.

Mom couldn't stop him, and I couldn't either. He had his gun, and he was heading up the hill to find Terry Coyne. Something monstrous was about to happen; the last shreds of my family had caught fire. Inside I flailed, but not for long. We didn't have long.

The clean, black-capped shape of the lighthouse loomed in the distance. Automatically, I turned to it. Like it was my new north star—like it was my last chance. I took a few, wobbling steps and called to Bailey.

"Take care of my mom," I shouted.

I didn't wait for an answer or let myself see the fear in Bailey's eyes. There was no time for it, no second guesses, no hesitations. It took me a few loping steps to get up to speed, but when I did, I burned with it. The untied braids in my hair came loose, and the wind whipped it all around my head.

When I'd had to escape, when I'd needed to get home, I'd hit the front door of the lighthouse running and come out on my parents' porch. Chest burning and throat raw with every hard breath, I hoped it worked the other way. I prayed and wished, and when I hit the shore, I screamed.

"I want to come back, Grey!" Splashing into the surf, my teeth chattered instantly. The cold gripped, razor sharp. But I kept wading out, salt in my mouth, blood in my throat.

"Grey, please!"

The muck pulled my shoes off; I fought to keep moving. I know I screamed for Grey again, that my voice tore through the clear, clear sky. Then the shallows dropped off, and I plunged beneath the waves. Below, it was frigid and peaceful, until I cut the water with frantic arms.

I sank, and I sank, still screaming.

TWENTY-ONE

Grey

I'm in no state to have callers, but Willa bursts through my door all the same.

She's soaked and maddened, and so exquisitely in focus. Cruelly, wonderfully, I see her in all her details. The freckle in one eye, the hundredshade of her red hair. What a pretty, pretty girl she is—when she's not raving.

Skidding to a stop, she holds up her hands. Broken music boxes surround her—there's a chance I lost my temper and smashed them all. Soul jars, music boxes, windows, too. Even the computer, for that was a rather disappointing window indeed.

Once I would have been embarrassed to receive a lady in my current state of undress. But cotton breeches and little else at least nod to my modesty and allow her to witness the whole of me in all my hideous natural state. I'm whitewash poured into a man-shaped glass. My head is—to be fair—not smooth, but quite round now. Quite evidently round, with all my hair shorn.

Her eyes widen as I approach; I frighten her. I should frighten her.

"Bring in the fog," she says. Her voice quavers. Her fingers curl into claws when I get closer. She really is horrified; wonderful! "Please, Grey, please. I'll stay if you want, I'll . . ."

I press a finger to her lips. "No, thank you."

"There's no time, please. Please. Help me, and I will make it up to you."

Spreading my arms wide, I shrug. I feel mercurial, just like the wind. The water. The sea, the sky. Flowing through the room, my feet cut a swath through shattered glass and twisted metal. I turn to her, and I would apologize, but there are no apologies left in me.

"It can't be done. I'm surrendering, you see."

Her eyes aren't black. They're brown, streaks of amber, flecks of green—that one dark spot that distracts me. There's a light on in there, behind those lashes. She's thinking, working, then suddenly, she throws herself at me. "Make me the Grey Man."

"Willa." I laugh. "That's fundamentally impossible."

"The Grey Lady," she shouts. "You know what I mean!"

She puts her hands on me; she shakes me. Oh, how I longed for that before today, though not like this. Not hard and furious. Would a gentle touch from her have been so very hard to offer? Delicate fingers to trace the illusory veins in my wrists, a loving touch to warm the back of my neck?

Yet, there is a spark. Just as the beacon above comes to life when it's needed, I feel something within me turn. Catching Willa's elbows, I seize it—before my muddled thoughts distract me entirely. It's a faery story after all, perhaps ending happily ever after for me. But this one does not begin once upon a time. It begins—

"Will you die for me?"

Willa shakes her head, stubborn to the last. "Not for you. For my family I will. But not for you."

It's within my grasp to toy with her. Torment her as she has tormented me. To hold out hope before her, just to snatch it away. I burn to do it; she'd deserve it. Instead, I cradle her face with my hand—I can be tender. I can be gentle.

I've been honest all along; my honor is mine and it's intact. Her suffering will come later. I've no need to exact revenge now. Not now.

In the end, I was right. She was thinking of me. She came to me. And now she sets me free.

Her lips are stone, but I press mine to them all the same. It's the only way I know how to give her this gift. At first, it seems I have only stolen a kiss. Then, a spike of light rips through me. My black-and-white world starts to bleed; my insubstantial body becomes flesh.

Dropping to my knees, I wrap my arms around myself to hold in the rising agony. I burst from the mist shell that's held me all these years. It's nothing but pain at first. I gasp and fall to my side. Music boxes jangle; they jab my flesh. They pierce me and I gasp. Breath hurts; the light hurts my eyes. My heart lurches into a pounding rage as sweat freshens me.

Writhing, I shudder and collapse again. I gape like a fish and gasp at air, real air, for the first time in a century.

And above me, Willa stands, washed in fog. Though I saw her in all her colors, she's grey now. White hair, grey lips, black eyes. She's a fearsome kind of beautiful, her edges trailing away as haze. Susannah was a delicate, fragile ghost. Willa is an avenging wraith—prepossessed and mighty.

She steps over my body, and a staircase appears as she raises her foot. The dregs of my reign melt like wet sugar. The music boxes, the shelves, all the disaster I wrought, fade with each step she takes. And when she disappears, I realize the silence in my head.

The cold on my skin.

The twist of hunger in my belly.

I could no more call the mist than I could fly. There's a Grey Lady in this tower now, a new mistress on Jackson's Rock. Though I've walked its shore a thousand times, my head aches imagining the borders of the island.

Struggling to my feet, I realize I'm no longer bare. Denim dungarees, a blue cotton shirt that clings to me. Shoes with laces, a curious jacket with a hood and zipper. Hunching into myself, I creep to the door. I close my eyes and say a soft prayer before I open it. Please let this be real, I murmur.

Then I step into the real world, a rocky shore that leads to the water—a boat waits for me there. It turns its bow to the distant shore. In the haze, its name wavers and changes. When the letters reshape themselves, it's then that I know I am free. They read

Charlie

TWENTY-TWO

Willa

It all makes sense now.

When the cold came on me, Grey faded to a ball of light and drifted away. The lighthouse became mine. Its walls shifted for me; the stairs spiraled down to meet my feet. The weight of the fog presses from every direction. It's like I'm part of it, and it's part of me.

Every single thing Grey told me swirls in my head—he wasn't wrong. This does feel primal. Old as the earth, old as time. Old as the sea and all its slumbering gods and goddesses, all its unknown and un-named monsters and miracles.

As I hurry to the lantern gallery, I see flickers of rooms to be. The library is there, but now with more maps of the ocean. Globes and tele-scopes, star charts and barometers—and gleaming in the middle of the room, a beautiful brass sextant. The stairs rattle under my feet; I keep going.

The room I woke in before is here too, and a bathroom with a claw-foot tub and a harbor view. It's all crazy pretty, and I'll explore it later. Part of me wonders what the kitchen will look like when I walk into it. Do I have a microwave? Can I watch TV?

Petty, unimportant thoughts. And I'll have forever to figure stuff like that out. Right now, I have to save what's left of my family.

Throwing open the gallery door, I don't catch my breath. I don't feel the slightest waver of mortal fear when I look down at the rocks. Already the tides in my body have turned. I'm not Willa Dixon anymore. I won't bleed. I can't leave. I'm the Grey Lady, and I'm all right with that.

Since it seems like I should, I raise my hands. Inside me, the push and the pull struggle for control. I choose pull. I yearn for it, thick blankets of white to spread over the water. Throughout Broken Tooth. Past my house and the church steeple. Between the stones in the graveyard. Beyond the Vandenbrook School and Jackie Ouelette's house on the hill.

On the far shore, there are so many lights. I understand that now too. All those lives, bobbing and dancing. Can't tell one from the other; all I know is that some are bright. Some are dim. But slowly, all of them are consumed by the wave of mist that I spill on them.

I reach until I feel my edges thinning. I pull; it's like a song. Like I have a new pulse—one that answers to the elements instead of my heart. Mist twines around my wrists and ankles; my hair is braided with it, my clothes woven from it. I master it, and it enslaves me. The push. The pull.

When I was lost in the fog, it took me only a few steps to realize I couldn't keep going. When I heard water, I knew I'd gone the wrong way. That's the kind of mist I call tonight. Thick and physical. The kind that leaves beads in your hair and a damp kiss on your skin. I'll hold it 'til dawn, though I'm not sure my dawn will be the same as the village's. Time passes differently here.

Still, I pull. More mist. More haze. In my veins and on the streets of Broken Tooth. I murmur with the song. I twist with it. As the beam cuts on behind me, the horn starts to call. I feel the waves pass through me, both light and sound.

Somewhere, Daddy's Girlfriend is theorizing why a day so clear turned so foggy all at once. Somewhere, I'm hoping—I bet my life—that my father pulled to the side of the road. It's not fit for ships or F-150s now. People are closing up their windows and doors, locking them tight. They know it isn't natural, this much fog, rolling in the wrong direction. This is everywhere, thick as flesh. It feels wrong, I know. But they don't have to worry.

I don't want to collect their souls. I don't want them to suffer. I don't want anyone to die tonight. Not even Terry Coyne.

My father knows what it's like to live by the sea. He's been in bar fights and regular fights; he's ridden out hurricanes and nor'easters. All these years, he's survived. No matter the hardship, he's survived and kept going, and kept our family going. And he's going to survive tonight, whether he wants to or not.

He doesn't realize it yet. It's a hard thing to truly understand. It doesn't matter if someone stands right in front of you and shouts it in your face. There are some things you have to realize. Internalize. More than understand—comprehend. Now that I have, I hope I'm giving my father the chance to understand it too.

It's not July twenty-third anymore.

TWENTY-TWO

Charlie

I didn't excel in my grammar studies, so I couldn't say it was *ironic*. But it did seem apt that the boat bearing my name cut through the mist to the other shore and left me stranded in the fog.

On hands and knees, I felt my way up to the boardwalk. Stones cut my palms. Rubbing the bright pain against my knees, I managed to warm myself as well. The hooded coat I woke with barely held the October cold at bay.

Anxious to run, I bounded a few steps, then stopped. Though I had mastered the fog for a century, it ignored my will now. At an arm's length, my fingertips were obscured by it. In me, there was an awareness of the village, that there were buildings quite close, but I couldn't see them.

As much as I longed to flee this coast, I sat instead. There was no use in escaping if the first thing I did was walk off a cliff. Besides, I had plenty to experience even without my eyes for the moment.

The air smelled different on this side of the water. Rotting bait, raw wood, salt water. There were other scents I couldn't place. Heavy, oily, greasy—and one I sensed not at all. With a deep breath, I closed my eyes and inhaled—but no, it wasn't there. The sweet tang of wood smoke eluded me entirely.

The last time I walked on real land, most homes kept a wood-burning stove for warmth and cooking alike. Though it was mainly imaginary, I'd had one in the lighthouse as well. Black and fat, radiating heat through its sides and issuing its smoke to wind around the lighthouse outside.

I had to wonder what the citizens of Broken Tooth had instead. In 1913, they were a poor, proud lot. Had they blossomed in a century? Willa always seemed so distracted among my things. Her world was a novel creation to me. Soon, I'd explore it all.

Settling in for a wait, I savored my curiosities and discomforts, for they were finally temporary. The wood dug into my backside. My back ached to sit without support. Hunger gnawed through me, and I felt distinctly gritty. Situations soon to be solved.

When the fog lifted, I'd find a chair, an inn, a public bath if there was no private one to be had.

Proof that I had been insubstantial before, I had a full head of hair once more. Instead of silvery white, it was brown again; I wondered if that meant my eyes were blue again. Stroking my own cheek, I sighed. I bore barely a day's stubble. My father's beard had never been particularly full either. No magic could change that destiny, it seemed.

I dug at the lump in my pocket and found a leather portfolio. It was no bigger than my hand, though thick. Flipping it open, I shivered. My eyes—indeed, blue—and my face as they once were stared back at me.

Thrusting a finger into the pocket that held it, I struggled to free the portrait.

The card was thin, pliable. Printed with green, grassy swirls and an etching of a mountain—it claimed my name was Charlie Walker. Which was true: Charles Leslie Walker. Named for neither grandfather; my parents hadn't cared for them.

I'd forgotten my birth date. The year was wrong on the card, 1995 instead of 1896, but the month and day . . . I could barely catch a breath. Vertigo left me unsettled. Stomach contracting, I felt as though my head were a bowl of well-stirred soup.

How could I have forgotten such an intimate detail? Why did it feel like such a blow to recover it?

As I thumbed through the rest of the folio, I listened to the ocean and the harbor bells, and the horn in the distance. It was rippingly fantastic to hear that sound from a mile away instead of right inside my own home. I was free. I was free! Cool wind enveloped me; the fog bathed me.

And I had, it seemed, one hundred seventeen dollars to my name. A princely sum—the bills strangely smooth, the portraits not quite familiar. Less green, more writing. They were smaller than the tender notes I remembered. Lifting them to my nose, I inhaled.

That was the same, at least.

I had no idea how long I sat on the boardwalk. I picked at my toes and leaned down to follow the progress of a line of ants. Once more through the portfolio in my pocket, then I stood and stretched. It seemed to me that the fog finally thinned, peeling away to reveal a hint of night.

The lighthouse beam swung over my head. It was like seeing a forsaken sweetheart. There was so much a part of me in that light. But that was over, a chapter completed. It made no difference to me how far it stretched, for I no longer needed to account for the souls beneath it.

The village slowly took shape. Lampposts soared above me, their bulbs glowing slightly orange. The poles buzzed; when I pressed my ears to them, I heard it distinctly. Electricity! For my mother's birthday, my father had installed two electric lights in our house. One in her kitchen, the other in the sitting room. Those lamps were dim compared with these creations.

Angled roofs and steep chimneys cast shadows within the haze. Windows glowed steadily—more electricity, I guessed. Absorbed in wonder, I walked up to a motorcar. That's what it had to be. It had wheels and glass lights, and curves like a jungle cat.

Hurrying to the next, I trailed my fingers along the hood. Suddenly, a Klaxon sounded, and I very nearly screamed. Hurrying away from that, I kept my admiration to examination by gaze alone. There were so many motorcars, as if each house on the street had at least one.

At the end of the block, I found a rusted horse cart. Motorized, I presumed, since it was branded with FORD on its rear. I'd been gone a century, but even I recognized that name. Circling it, I marveled at its width and breadth. Then I stopped short when I saw a different face from mine in the front window.

Inside, a man rubbed drowsily at his neck, sleeping soundly. When he shifted, a shotgun slid down the seat beside him. Those hadn't changed greatly in the interval either. The black barrel gleamed; the wood stock shone with polish.

Trembling, I backed away from the cart, then turned to hurry up the street. I was new and freshly living again. I didn't care to enrage a man who traveled with arms in the open. I passed houses and listened to the strange sounds issuing from them as I walked.

I reached the edge of town, where I found an establishment

with a flickering-light sign outside; it promised a vacancy at the inn.

When I pushed open the glass doors, I had to shield my eyes. The lights were unbearably bright in the lobby. Moving pictures played on a box on the counter, not quite like my computer, but similar. A floral scent overwhelmed me, and when I approached, I quite frightened the young man behind the counter.

"I need a room for the night, one with a washbasin," I said. I reached for my portfolio and ignored the lying birth date on my portrait card.

"Jesus, dude," he said, slowly taking to his feet. "Where the hell did you come from?"

Considering the question, I offered him my card. And then finally I told him, "Oh, it's best if we just say another place. Another time."

"Whatever," he muttered, and reached for a key.

TWENTY-THREE

Willa

When I finally set the mist free, I collapse. What's strange is, though my knees clang against the gallery floor, I don't really feel it. There's an echo that almost feels like pain, but I'm too tired to examine it. Time is different here. I hope I smothered Broken Tooth long enough.

I think it's night, but I'm not sure about that, either. Rising, I find the staircase waiting for me. All I want is sleep, or rest, or whatever. I have a lot to learn about being the Grey Lady. As much as Grey thinks he told me, there's a metric buttload to still figure out.

The one thing I do remember is that I get a present at breakfast. That I get to wish for what I want to fill my plate. The staircase rattles, then opens into my bedroom. It's exactly the same as before. White net canopy, green witch balls in the window . . . pictures of my family on the wall. Of the Jenn-a-Lo. Of my used-to-bes.

Straightening the picture of me and Levi on the boat, I make my present wish. Breakfast can be whatever. Pancakes and sausage and home fries, I guess. But when I wake up, I want proof that my father, my family, is okay. I want to know that I did the right thing. A little proof that it was a good trade, my forever for my father's present.

I lie on the bed, my feet still on the floor. I don't feel my heart beating. I breathe, but I think that's only because I want to. When I stop, my chest doesn't fill up. I don't get hot. Or panicked. My throat doesn't tighten, and I'm not struggling to inhale.

This is real. I really did it.

I close my eyes. I do not dream.

When I woke, morning sunlight streamed through the window.

My witch balls were gone. My pictures. All the little things that made that room mine. I lay on the floor and shivered. The wood was rough and old. Chewing up my elbows, it groaned when I pushed myself to my feet.

A splinter slipped into my palm, and I cursed. It was a small, bright pain. Kinda weird, all things considered. Kinda raw. As I headed for the door, I wrapped my arms around myself.

I wasn't sure what was going on, because Grey never said the lighthouse looked like this to him. Dilapidated and broke down.

Mold on the walls. Spiders in the corners. My back was killing me, and my mouth tasted like somebody camped in it.

I didn't need a mirror to know my hair was a janked-up mess and my clothes were wrinkled from sleeping in them. That was the one thing about Grey that always fascinated me. How perfect he looked all the time. I thought maybe I was doing this wrong. Maybe it was like making jewelry. I could follow along, but it was obvious I wasn't a natural at it.

The stairs scared me. Rusted, the frame gaped away from the wall. Old bolts scraped in the holes, sending a dusting of plaster snow to filter to the floor. The planks that made up the steps — the ones that were still there — looked eaten up. Termites or time or something. I couldn't believe it, because this was supposed to be all me. All my wishes and dreams.

A falling-down deathtrap? That was what the lighthouse decided I wanted? I wondered if there was a union I could talk to. A Monster and Faery Local 223, where I could complain about the condition of my haunt.

I laughed, and it echoed. Like the place was empty, that kind of echoing. And I slowly made my way downstairs, where the kitchen should have been. Or the music-box room. Or whatever room ought to be there at that particular minute. But there was nothing. Just an empty lighthouse.

Old gauges and pipes clung to the wood pillars, rust tears

streaking beneath them. Broken windows let a constant, cold stream of air inside. That wind whispered, going around and around, echoing all the way to the top. Again, that echo, hollow and evacuated.

When I tipped my head back, the stairs stayed put. They spiraled up. Even when I turned my back to them and stole a look from the corner of my eye, they were there. Creeping to the door, I reached for the knob, then hesitated.

It didn't seem fair that Grey got everything he wanted and I got a tore-up lighthouse that looked its age. None of it seemed fair, actually. That he got stuck here because he was a fool for love. That I'd be stuck here for trying to save my family.

Not that superstition had to do with fair. Legends, either. That was the point, really, of all those once-upon-a-time stories—to warn us. To save us from quirk and whim and random chance. Happenstance. To protect us from things beyond our control.

It was bad luck to let a woman or a pig onboard; you'd sink a boat if you set the deck hatch upside down. Eat a stranger's food, spend half the year in the underworld. A poison apple means you sleep forever.

Twisting the knob, I threw the door open and saw a whole new Jackson's Rock. Into the forest, I shivered at the cold—but only the cold. Everything smelled fresh—the balsam firs and jack pines sweetened every step. As I walked the clearing path,

I heard just what I would have expected to. Birdsong. Leaves rustling as squirrels and raccoons traipsed through.

At the peak, I stopped. Above me, clear blue sky stretched above the naked, nearly winter trees. Below me, just down the western side of the island, I made out a blueberry barren. That would be something, come summertime.

Walking again, I picked up a few of the tiny shells that littered the path. They cut my thumb and jingled in my pocket. When I broke through to the other side, the sun shone like new gold. It capped the stony shore, gleaming across its expanse.

The terns we always thought lived on the island were there, their nests anyway. A couple of petrels stretched twig-thin legs and skimmed across the water. When they landed, they waddled a few steps across the cobble beach and looked my way. Their masked faces showed no surprise or concern.

Before, Jackson's Rock had been a dark, dead place. Now it lived. Approaching the water, I wondered if I would shear apart if I stepped into it, the way Grey described. What were my limits now? How much of this world was mine to have, and how much of it could I only watch?

Wading out, I found the water so cold, it burned. My skin tightened and ached. It spread to my scalp; it made my ears ring. I kept going deeper, until I had to swim. Until I had to catch my breath.

Had to.

The blast of a horn startled me. Splashing back toward shore, I threw my hair out of my face as a Coast Guard cutter streamed closer. A loudspeaker came on—usually a sound a lobsterman didn't care to hear. But the woman's voice that crackled over it was *beautiful.*

"Stay right there. We're coming to get you."

TWENTY-THREE

Charlie

After two days cocooned in my inn, I had to get some air.

Surrounded by electricity, lit by a moving-picture box, I gorged myself on visions of the world as it had become. I sat beneath hot running water that never seemed to fade. The rhythm of motorcars and people coming and going lulled me to sleep.

But I'd been asleep a hundred years. I'd had enough of it. The realization that I had no one left pained me more in skin than in mist. It was an agonizing solitude. And a hundred dollars didn't last nearly so long as it might have done once.

My only thought was to catch a boat headed for Boston. There, I could search for the remains of my life interrupted.

Packing my meager belongings took but a moment. Then I let myself out and smiled at the sun and the sky, at lungs that took real breaths. To be sure, bittersweetness ruled each moment. But I was alive again, and sometimes life was suffering.

Turning myself to the shore, I hurried on my errand. It seemed entirely improbable, as I walked through the morning sunlight, that the first face I saw was Willa's. Nevertheless, it was so. Not a memory of it, nor a replica. No hallucination or wishful thinking.

It was she, standing on the wharf with a blanket wrapped round her shoulders.

Some sort of uniformed officer put a hand on her back and guided her to the pavement. A deep-plucked emotion stirred in me, a bewildering concoction of both fear and longing. Past her, in the distance, the lighthouse cut a fine silhouette against a clear sky.

There was nothing there anymore.

If I said that I simply knew it to be true, it would be a lie. There were signs—I could gaze at Jackson's Rock and had no inclination to look away. Once shrouded by mists, the island was clear and bright. Birds flew over it. Waters flowed to it. There was nothing there anymore.

Rubbing at the ache in my chest, I turned to watch Willa. I'd been made flesh with her sacrifice. Humiliating, indeed, that she'd denied me until the end. But as I followed her with my gaze, I blushed. Shame, for my madness. My desperation. For failing to realize that every curse has a breaking point.

True love's kiss, or the tears of an innocent. Neither applied, in my estimation. Folding my hands behind my back, I watched as a woman leapt from a motorized horse cart. A man slid from the other side, and *he* was familiar indeed.

Silvery hair, but shot with red, I'd seen him sleeping in that very horse cart, his shotgun at hand. Willa crashed into him, burying her face against his chest. His hands wavered uneasily, then finally fell on her back. The woman closed the circle around her.

Reaching for a nearby bench, I had to sit down.

This was Willa's family.

The one left gaping with her brother's death, the one that drove her to beg at my feet to become the Grey Lady. In a hundred years, I hadn't felt the pain of a knot in my throat. Nor the sudden burn of tears that somehow also occluded a good, deep breath.

It was never the kiss or the tears that broke the curse. It was the pure heart behind them. A pure heart I'd never had. A selfless longing I'd never felt.

Even at that moment, watching Willa's reunion, I had not a bit of selflessness in me. I wanted her to raise her head so I could meet her eyes, and she, mine. She was the only soul left in the world who knew me.

But she never looked back.

EPILOGUE

On my graduation day, I still had superstition, but I had hope, too.

Vandenbrook always held commencement in the school's ballroom. That was one of the nice things about going to an old Victorian mansion instead of some brick building built for learning: it had pretty touches.

Stained glass that streamed colors over us, just twenty of us, as we sat in our caps and gowns. Bathed in scarlet and gold, we listened to the principal talk too long. Bailey's valedictorian speech was just right.

I wasn't gonna tell anybody that her goodbye to senior year had done double duty as the essay that got her accepted into three different colleges, including the one she finally picked.

UGA, down in Georgia—Cait decided on USC in Los Angeles. They were gonna try to make it work long-distance.

We got our diplomas, and I posed with Seth and Bailey, for all three sets of our parents. Just like he promised, Seth was heading to Seattle. Not so much a guitar and a dream. Just a different life he wanted to try on. I kissed his cheek and sent him on his way.

After the cake and punch and a couple of rounds of crying from my mom, Bailey took off with me. Her sad, broke-down truck had one last job to do before she consigned it to the truck graveyard.

In the lot behind my house, *my* boat sat on a trailer. She was just a twenty-four-foot keel, nothing I could fish from. But I wouldn't be fishing for a while, and that's not why I bought her. It took a year and a half to clean her up and get her seaworthy, but she was finally there.

Hooking the trailer to Bailey's truck, I hopped in her cab for one last time. Her face was a little red from holding the parking brake back so hard.

"You never were gonna get those brakes fixed, were you?"

She blew me a kiss and dropped the brake. "Not for any woman, no ma'am."

It wasn't a long drive to the shore, though backing the trailer to the water was more exciting than it had to be. For a minute, I thought we were gonna commit Bailey's truck to a sea burial.

She managed to stop it at the last minute, then cut the engine.

"There's a coast in Georgia," she said as she hopped out. She came around to help me with the chains. "I don't know how far it is from Athens, but I'm probably going to buy a car when I get down there."

Grinning at her, I steadied myself against the hull. "With brakes?"

"When's the last time I told you to kiss it?"

With a laugh, we both moved at the same time to set my boat in the water. I had new plans to sail the coast. To see more of the world than Broken Tooth, Maine. I'd come back in the springtime, to help Daddy get the traps ready for the season, and to teach his temporary sternman how to do my job.

And when I got my license back, I'd take my place. These waters were my waters; this village was my home. The legacy still mattered. I was gonna work the stern of the *Jenn-a-Lo* until Daddy retired. Then I'd step into the wheelhouse, her new captain.

I'd be able to do it knowing that I had seen other places and lived other lives and still chosen this one. Three hundred years of Dixons had fished these waters; three hundred more waited. I didn't want my initials to be the last set on the banister at Vandenbrook.

"I'm not crying for you," Bailey informed me, wiping her face.

I hugged her, and bumped our foreheads together. Then I

pinched her as I let go. "That's to give you something to cry about."

That night, we had a bonfire on Jackson's Rock. The whole senior class, and let's be honest, most of the juniors and sophomores, too. Nobody could remember why we'd never done it before.

Since you could only sail onto the south side of the island, we were hidden in the cove. There was plenty of downed wood to burn, and instead of cold, damp caves for secret kisses, there was an abandoned lighthouse.

I stayed until the stars shifted to midnight. Until the waters were clear and smooth and I could see the mainland shore glimmering in the distance. Setting off across perfect seas, not on a Friday, I was whole. Happy. Alive.

Hours slipped by, and as I passed the cliff over Daggett's Walk, I could have sworn I saw a figure standing on the shore. He was a pang and a light—I squinted to try to make him out.

Somebody was there, for sure, leaning against a truck, while someone else waited in the cab. The watcher's face was familiar but *not* familiar. Impressions of shadows that came together to shape a thin mouth and keen eyes. I couldn't know him for sure. But for some reason, I thought I might.

It was only a moment, and I sailed on by. I had too many

things to think about to lose myself wondering. To spend time adding up an expression, matching it to a memory. I was my own captain, and I had to think about the stars and the seas and my path through them.

But if I hadn't been imagining things—if he really was that ghost I'd known in the lighthouse—it was all right. I didn't have to stop or wave. No need to say hello. I wasn't sure I'd ever need to speak to him again.

I was changed, and he was necessary, but it wasn't that kind of magic. Not gold ink calligraphy swirling across the page, a delicate, transcendent *the end*. But he was *something*.

A boat's name was its charm. It was full of superstition like everything else—remembrance, penance, prayer. In our fleet, there was the *Boondocks*, where Mal Eldrich hailed from. The *Jenn-a-Lo*, for my daddy's wife. *Lazarus* belonged to Zoe Pomroy, and she sure as hell had brought it back from the dead when she bought it off the side of the road for fifteen pounds of blueberries.

The night was sweet with lilac blooms; clear skies over clear waters. Singing with my engine, the wind wound through the trees and crept into my cabin. My belly was full; I was warm. I had a direction. The whole world waited.

I sailed on to my destiny on the *Levi Grey*.

ACKNOWLEDGMENTS

Professional thanks to Julie Tibbott—never was there a finer editor—and my wonderful agent, Jim McCarthy. Though we have yet to watch a good show together, I remain ever hopeful.

Foundational thanks to Mandy Hubbard for helping me find the high in the concept, LaTonya Dargan for bringing the legal science up in my house, and Colonel Joe Fessenden from the Marine Patrol for clarifying the consequences of cutting gear and *not* getting away with it.

Extraordinary thanks to Abigail Luchies (@Aluchies), Kelly Jensen (@catagator), Susan Dee (@literacydocent), and Laura Phelps (@elfhelps) for Twittersourcing the perfect full-time Mainechecker. This is why teachers and librarians rock, y'all.

Wild, enthusiastic thanks and adoration to Emma Wallace, for being that perfect, full-time Mainechecker. You made this book a million times better, Emma. Thank you so much! Much gratitude and appreciation to Rick and Diane Wallace as well, for lending their daughter to a strange author from Indiana.

Lovey author thanks go to Christine Johnson for massaging the partial, R. J. Anderson for reading and cheerleading, Deva Fagan for checking my Maine in the early stages, and Carrie Ryan and Sarah MacLean for helping me find the magic. Thanks and smoochies to Sarah Rees Brennan for the handholding and lamenting.

Forever and ever thanks to Jason Walters, who insisted I needed an office and refused to stop until I had one. Thank you for being my champion and my hero, always.

Finally, Wendi Finch, my muse and my hetero-lifemate, who knows that the last ferry will take us to Maine, back to Maine, always to Maine.